Israel Longworth

Life of S.G.W. Archibald

Israel Longworth

Life of S.G.W. Archibald

ISBN/EAN: 9783337333737

Printed in Europe, USA, Canada, Australia, Japan

Cover: Foto ©Raphael Reischuk / pixelio.de

More available books at **www.hansebooks.com**

LIFE

OF

S. G. W. ARCHIBALD,

BY

ISRAEL LONGWORTH.

.

HALIFAX, N.S.,
1881

.

PRINTED BY
S. F. HUESTIS,
HALIFAX, N.S.

PREFACE.

The writer of this Memoir had occassion, while reparing a History of the County of Colchester, to make some rather minute investigations into the circumstances connected with the first settlement of Truro—and its progress as it developed from a straggling hamlet in the wilderness, to the thriving and bustling town which it is at this day. In doing so, he was struck with the prominent part taken in its affairs by the members of one family, a family which has been connected with the town from its earliest history. Four generations of this family in lineal descent have been members of the Nova Scotian Assembly. The subject of our memoir, his father, his grandfather, and his eldest son have sat in the Assembly as representatives of the people. We doubt if the same can be said of any other Nova Scotian family.

Other sons of the same gentleman, have occupied distinguised positions outside the Province. One, who died in 1876, was, at the time of his death, a Judge in the High Court of Justice in England. Another, who still lives, is Consul General for Great Britain in the United States of America.

Of each of these sons we published some account, about a year ago. At the time we intended to complete the series by a memoir of their father, which we hoped to be able to prepare shortly afterwards. We soon found however, that a biography of the father was a very different task from that of either of the sons. In preparing the previous sketches, we had to relate events mainly of a personal or professional character—to tell of the progress of two able men on their way to distinction in different countries till they rose, one in the Metropolis of the Old World, to be a Judge in the Queen's Bench ; the other, in the Metropolis of the New World, to fill one of the most arduous posts in the Imperial service—and to fill it in a way to elicit the marked approval of the Sovereign. There was another broad distinction between the former work and that in which we have since engaged. Then, we had to deal with events of comparatively recent date, and of which abundant records remained. But a memoir of the father takes us back to a period, and to events, comparatively unknown or forgotten. The materials for such a task are difficult of access. They are scattered in different places. Living memory does not go back to the early, or even to the middle, period of his life. Tradition, as is usual, has blended much of fiction with a small amount of fact. This rendered it all the more necessary to use care, and to spend time, in searching for the truth. When we first thought of the work, we had little time at command. However, by devoting the spare hours of a not idle year, to this service, we have been able to gather a considerable body of materials, which we have endeavoured to throw into shape. If we had had more leisure, we should have been able perhaps to make our little book more presentable, but we would fondly hope that even in the imperfect shape in which it now appears, it will not be without interest in the eyes of our fellow countrymen. Should it be otherwise, the blame must rest on us. If it fails to interest, the fault is in the treatment, not in the subject. Whatever be the reception accorded to our effort, we may say that it has been our steady aim throughout to deal fairly and impartially with the memory of one of Nova Scotia's most gifted sons.

THE AUTHOR.

Truro, April 23rd., 1881.

CONTENTS.

CHAPTER I.

FROM BIRTH IN 1777 TO ELECTION TO ASSEMBLY IN 1806.

Description of Truro in 1777. First settlement of the Brothers Archibald. David the Grand-father. Samuel the Father. Death of Father. Stories of early life. Residence with Grand-father. Letter of introduction from his sister Elizabeth Elliot to his cousin Mrs. Lamb. Her kindness. At School at Haver-hill and Andover. Intended Profession. Change. Study of law. Marriage. Appointed Judge of Probate. Admitted to Bar. Elected to Assembly.　　　　　　　　　1—10

CHAPTER II.

Politics in 1806. Sir John Wentworth. William Cottnam Tonge elected Speaker and rejected. Mr. Wilkins becomes Speaker. Mr. Archibald's first motion in the Assembly. Takes charge of Road Questions. Religion in 1806. Kings College. Croke's Test Clauses. Controversy between two Bishops. Mr. McCulloch intervenes. He keeps a school. What followed. 11—20

CHAPTER III.

1817 to 1825.

Mr. Archibald as an Advocate. King *vs.* Sawers. King *vs.* Holland. King *vs.* Forrester. - - - - - 21—38

CHAPTER IV.

Interest in Agriculture. Manufacturing Operations. Visit to England. Appointed Chief Justice of P. E. I. Visits the Island. Address of Grand Inquest. Dinner at Pictou. Dinner and address at Truro. Made Solicitor General in place of Mr. Robie promoted. Chosen Speaker. Election of 1826. Again chosen Speaker. Non-residence in P. E. I. Aims at Chief Justiceship of N. S. Claims of different candidates. Changes impending. Grounds of Blowers' retention of office. Sir Peregrine Maitland's perplexities. Correspondence with Sir John Coape Sherbrooke. The misdirected letter.　　　　　39—54

CHAPTER V.

The Brandy Question. Death of George IV. Dissolution of the
House.   55—88

CHAPTER VI.

President reports to Colonial Minister. Speaker does same.
President writes to Under Secretary of Colonies. Reply. Mr.
Archibald declines Judgeship. Council's friends disappointed
with Mr. Archibald's course. Reasons assigned. Curious letter in the Free Press. Conjectures as to its authorship. Dis-
section of letter. Consideration of reasons assigned by letter
writer.   89—97

CHAPTER VII.

Election of 1830. Candidates. Mr. Archibald's speech at Truro.
Meeting of House. Death of Attorney General Uniacke. Of-
fice kept open. Passage of Revenue Bill. Lord Goderich's
Despatch. Mission of Judge Halliburton to England. Mr.
Archibald appointed acting Attorney General. Visits England.
Judge Halliburton's and Mr. Archibald's race in England.
Attentions in England. Marquis of Lansdown's offer. Rejected.
Lord Goderich proposes changes in Judiciary. House refuse.
Lord Goderich to Administrator. Conclusion of question of
Chief Justiceship. Correspondence thereon. Remarks on
mode of day for obtaining promotion. Reaction after 1830.
State of public opinion in 1835 and '36. Joe Warner's Letters.
General Election of 1836. Mr. Logan's candidacy. Mr.
Archibald's speeches at Truro. Returned to Assembly. 98—120

CHAPTER VIII.

Curious results of Election. General effect of same. Disappearance of old members. First appearance of new men afterwards
attaining eminence. Re-elected Speaker. Illness. Mr. Smith
appointed Speaker temporarily. Failure of crops in 1836. Mr.
Dodd brings a Bill before the House to keep grain and potatoes
in the Province. Mr. Archibald's speech in its favor. Mr.
Young opposes the measure. His death. Resolutions transmitted to England. Reply. Rebellion in Lower Canada. Troops
sent from Halifax to Montreal. Public Meeting at Halifax.
Resolutions for relief of Soldiers' families. Patriotic speech of
Mr. Archibald. Mr. Howe's vindication of the loyalty of the
Liberals of Nova Scotia. Meeting of House in 1838. Appointment of Lord Durham as Lord High Commissioner and Governor General of British North America. His Report on the sit-

uation of the Provinces. An act of his administration attacked in the Lords by Lords Brougham and Lyndhurst. The Ministry disallow the ordinances complained of. Lord Durham's hasty return to England. Lord John Russel becomes Colonial Secretary. Mr. C. Poulett Thompson appointed Governor General. Resolutions of 1839. Delegates sent by House to England. Met by Council's Delegates. Lord John Russell's despatch of 16th October, 1839, as to tenure of Office. Additions to Executive Council from Assembly. Vote of want of Confidence in Government. Resignation of Hon. J. B. Uniacke. Subsequent action of House. Vote against Sir Colin Campbell. Mr. Archibald's views on that vote. The Governor General at Halifax. Lord Falkland becomes Governor of Nova Scotia. New appointments to Council. Election of 1840. Mr. Archibald re-turned for Colchester without opposition.   121—149

CHAPTER IX.

New Speaker. Reasons for Mr. Archibalds disqualification. Other Candidates equally disqualified. Two members of same Government contending for Speakership. Mr. Uniacke a member of Government moves resolution touching repeal of Union with Cape Breton. Resolution complimentary to Mr. Archibald adopted unanimously. Offered offices of Master of Rolls and Judge of Admiralty Court. Accepts. Mr. Archibald as Judge. Address at Truro. His Country seat. His habits at Truro. Hospitality. His Humour.   150—159

CHAPTER X.

Success as a Judge. Failing health. Death. Meeting of Bar Society. Speech of Chief Justice. Address of Condolence. Meeting of Colchester people on his death. Eulogium of Mr. Howe. Examination of charges against Mr. Archibald as a public man. Mr. Howes views upon them. Mr Archibald in his social relations. Death of his first wife. Account of his second wife. Sir Charles Pollack and Sir T. D. Archibald. Mr. Archibald's love for the sacred Scriptures. Anecdote related by Rev. Mr. Morton. Thoughts of writer in concluding Memoir.   160—179

LIFE OF
S. G. W. ARCHIBALD.

CHAPTER I.

FROM BIRTH IN 1777 TO ELECTION TO ASSEMBLY IN 1806.

Description of Truro in 1777. First settlement of the Brothers Archibald. David the Grand-father. Samuel the Father. Death of Father. Stories of early life. Residence with Grand-father. Letter of introduction from his sister Elizabeth Elliot to his cousin Mrs. Lamb. Her kindness. At School at Haverhill and Andover. Intended Profession. Change. Study of law. Marriage. Appointed Judge of Probate. Admitted to Bar. Elected to Assembly.

The Town of Truro, (or, as it might be called in reference to the time when the subject of our memoir was born there, the settlement of Truro,) has reason to be proud of having given birth to Samuel George William Archibald. He was a man who in his day filled an infinite variety of parts, and filled them all with credit. He had great and versatile talents. In any country, he would have attained distinction; in his own, he rose, step by step, till he had filled in turn almost every office in the Province, which could be held by a lawyer or a politician, He shone in social, as in professional and political life, He charmed every body by the amenity and courtesy of his manner. His kindness of heart, his vivacity and good humour, diffused pleasure wherever he appeared. His keen sense of the ridiculous extracted endless amusement from the dullest of incidents. In the wittiest and most brilliant circles, he was himself the wittiest and most brilliant of the party.

Surely a man of such accomplishments must have started in life with many adventitious aids; he must have enjoyed a superior education; he must have formed his manners in high social circles; he must have sharpened his wit and refined his taste by early association with men of culture and ability.

Let us look at the facts. When Mr. Archibald was born, Truro was a straggling village on the banks of the Salmon River. Barely seventeen years had passed since the first English settler had set foot in it. The original forest was still standing, except where a few small clearings around the houses showed an inconsiderable encroachment on the wilderness. Log fences lined highways, on which stumps of the original trees could be seen, and, near where the Salmon River is now bridged, the settlers crossed it in a log canoe. The inhabitants, to be sure, were intelligent and respectable. The race had come originally from Scotland, and had been since the reign of William 3rd, settled in the north of Ireland. The new settlers retained and brought with them the creed and the virtues derived from their Scotch ancestry. They were fairly instructed in the elementary branches of learning, and they strove to maintain, in the second country of their adoption, the principles and habits which had distinguished them in the first. They were a pious and God-fearing people, industrious and honest, but more noted for force of character than for polish or refinement. Among such a people, and with such surroundings, the subject of our memoir was born on the fifth day of February, 1777.

Four brothers of the name of Archibald were among

the first settlers of Truro. They were the ancestors of men of that name now scattered over Nova Scotia and the neighbouring Provinces and States. They arrived in Truro in the autumn of 1762. David Archibald, the eldest of the four, was the leading mind in the new settlement. Immediately on his arrival, he was made a Justice of the Peace and Major of Militia. Truro, then settled by fifty families, was entitled to send a Member to the Assembly. David Archibald was returned as the first Representative.

Samuel, the eldest son of David, was born in Londonderry, in Ireland. He accompanied his father and uncles when they came to Truro, and was then twenty years of age. He had received a fair education, was a good speaker and writer, and an active man of business. He had many of the peculiarities of appearance and manner which distinguished his son, the subject of our memoir.

In 1775, Samuel Archibald was returned as representative for Truro, and two years afterwards again returned for a second term. He was member for Truro at the time of his death, which took place on the fifteenth day of February, 1780.

He was engaged in business as a purchaser and shipper of lumber. On the 13th December, 1779, he left Passamaquaddy, in the Schooner Zephion, Jonathan Ingersoll Master, with a cargo of lumber, the property of himself, his brother Thomas, and Doctor John Harris of Truro, on a voyage to Bermuda. This was before the close of the war with the Old Colonies. On the voyage, while off Bermuda, the ship and cargo were seized as American property by a British Privateer, "The Admiral Barrington," Charles Sloane Commander, and carried into Nevis, one of the Leeward Islands. There the

ship and cargo were libelled in the Admiralty Court.
A defence was put in. Eventually the Court ordered the
property to be restored to the owners, but so far as Mr.
Archibald was concerned the decree came too late. He
had been seized with fever on his arrival, and died the
very day after the Decree had passed ordering restora-
tion of the property.

Thomas Archibald, another of the part owners, left
Nova Scotia some time subsequently to look after the
property, but was never heard of again. Nothing was
ever received from ship or cargo.

This sad event left the family, which consisted of a
widow and five children, in great difficulties. The eldest
of the children was then under ten years of age.

Samuel George William, the third son, was about
three years old. The family continued to live with their
mother on the old homestead, known as the Town's end
farm on Salmon River, the title of which was in David,
father of deceased. In 1783, the widow married John
McKeen, Esq., and shortly afterwards removed with him
to St. Marys. Thenceforth little Sammy, as he was called, lived with his grandfather till he was fifteen years
old. During this period his exuberant spirits and great
love of fun and frolic, distinguished him among the boys
of the place, as the merriest and most mischievous of the
lot. In Truro and the neighborhood, numerous stories
are in circulation of pranks played by him in early youth.
Many of these no doubt are fabulous, but like most
myths, they have some foundation in fact. It is said
that when he was about twelve years old, his grandfather
gave him, on some special occasion, a new homespun
jacket as a present, with particular injunctions to be careful of it, and to keep it clean. Sammy was delighted

with the jacket, but having a fancy to see how it would look on his big dog, he caught the animal and putting his forepaws through the sleeves, he buttoned the jacket over the dog's back, and then stood off to admire him. The dog however, not liking the operation, made for the door, and ran into a field from which potatoes had just been dug, and which was then very wet. He rushed about trying to get rid of his garment, but without success. At last he was captured, but the jacket was saturated with mud and dirt, and little Sammy probably received from his grand-father what he well deserved for the prank.

Another story told of him is, that he tried to put a pig into a mill race, to see whether the animal could swim, but that, missing his footing, he went in himself, and was carried down the race, and passed over the wheel into the stream below, not very much hurt but a good deal frightened. There must have been some foundation for this story. He was often chaffed about it in after life. He was told that he ought to be better than the rest of his family, inasmuch as he had been ground over again. On one occasion on the hustings, he said himself jokingly in reference to some complaint made against him, " You know, David, I have been through the Mill." " Yes, Sammy," was the reply, " but there is bran in you yet."

Another story of his early propensity to mischief has reference to the profession of which he was afterwards tô be a distinguished ornament. The Court Room at Truro was ceiled with boards overhead. There was an old lawyer then in practice there, who was no favorite with the boys. He was surly in temper and not always sober. When he addressed the Court he stood on a particular spot in front of the Judge. Just over his head, in the loft, our youth had bored a gimlet hole in the ceiling. This he stopped with a peg, and round the peg piled some very find sand. He had arranged with a confederate, to be informed by signs when the lawyer rose to speak. On receiving the signal he pulled the peg, and forthwith a gentle shower of fine sand descended through the hole. So soon as it lighted on the bald head beneath, the peg was replaced, and there was nothing to show the source of the descending shower. Again and again, whenever the speech was begun, the peg was withdrawn, and the sand descended from an invisible point. The astonished advocate, when he felt the sand, would look up, but could see nothing but the mist of the descending shower. At length the old man could stand it no longer. He left his client and his cause, and took refuge in a tavern in the neighborhood. There he resorted to his usual consolation in time of trouble.

On another occasion little Sammy nearly scared his grand-mother out of her wits, by setting her spinning-wheel in motion from the cellar, by a horse hair attachment through a hole in the floor.

We will not vouch for the truth of any or either of these stories. They are hardly worthy, even if true, of being inserted in a biography, but they show the irrepressible love of fun and merriment which distinguished the subject of our memoir from his boyhood. A steady flow of spirits enabled him, all through life, to mingle work with play. By the different currents, thus given to his thoughts, he relieved the cares and anxieties of life, and was enabled to perform more and better work, than if his mind had always been kept running in the same groove.

It is a subject of marvel that a boy, with such a spirit of mischief, did not get into serious scrapes. He was saved from such a result by his strong common sense, a quality which distinguished him through life, a quality not always combined with great wit and humor. He never carried his mischief beyond a certain point.

The boy's early days, passed under his grandfather's roof, were probably not altogether wasted. There were schools, such as they were, in those days. The new settlers, fairly instructed in youth in the common branches, spared no pains to establish such schools as the condition of the country permitted. As regards religious education, they had hardly reached their new home before they made preparations to secure the sacred privileges enjoyed by them in the Old World. In six years from the day of their arrival, they had erected a Meeting House, the frame of which was of such dimensions that it could be raised only by the united efforts of every grown person in the place, men and women. Two years later they forwarded a call to the Rev. Daniel Cock, a Presbyterian Minister, then settled in Greenock. He had accepted the call, and been settled in Truro some five years before the birth of Mr. Archibald. His influence would be felt in the schools. The education of youth is a matter which every Scotch Minister considers of special importance. Be that as it may, any person who has listened to the speeches or read the compositions of Mr. Archibald in after life, cannot fail to perceive evidences of early culture, in the style and character of his language. Still the education which could have been procured in Nova Scotia, a century ago, could not have been of a very superior kind. We had then neither Colleges nor High Schools.

Elizabeth Elliot, the oldest daughter of the deceased Samuel Archibald, seems to have been a woman of much force of character. She had, after the second marriage of her mother, constituted herself in a special manner the guardian of her youngest brother. It was by her advice, and with the assistance she was able to procure from friends and relatives, that he was sent to the United States for his education.

The widow of Samuel Archibald had many relatives in Massachusetts. Her husband had married her there, and she had left behind her, when she came to her new home, several brothers and sisters. An affectionate intercourse subsisted between the different branches of the family in Massachusetts and Nova Scotia. Rosanna Duncan was the daughter of one of the widows' brothers. She had recently married Mr. Lamb, the father of Thomas Lamb, the well known Boston Banker, who is still alive, at the venerable age of 84, and who is a fine specimen, physically and mentally, of a gentleman of the olden time.

When the boy was sent to the States, he took with him a letter of introduction, from his sister Elizabeth Elliot, to his cousin Mrs. Lamb. It bears date the 30th October, 1792, and commends the youth to the kind consideration and protection of his cousin. The letter is before us as we write, and, alike in language and tone, is creditable to the excellent woman who wrote it.

Nothing could be kinder than the reception the boy met with, when he presented himself with his sister's letter. He was taken into the family of his cousin and treated in all respects as one of themselves.

He attended the Academy at Haverhill, Massachusetts, for several years. From there he went to Andover, then, as now, the site of an excellent Academy. It had.

been for many years in successful operation, and was in great repute in the United States, and in the Provinces.

While there, he diligently improved his time by close and constant study. He returned to his home towards the close of 1796, with a sound academical education, well qualified to take his part, with credit, in the business of life.

On his return, it was his first intention to proceed to Scotland to be ordained a Presbyterian Minister. All his early associations were connected with the Presbyterian Body. His grand-father was the first Elder of the Presbyterian Church in this Province, and took a leading part in religious, as well as secular matters. He it was who originated the proceedings for bringing the Reverend Daniel Cock to Truro. He was the first subscriber to the instrument which secured the minister's salary, and up to the close of his life, he took a leading part in every movement connected with the Presbyterian Church. Brought up under these influences, the young man was early impressed with religious feelings. He had devoted some time at Andover to theological studies. Certain it is that all through life he displayed great familiarity with the scriptures. He quoted them with facility and accuracy; occasionally, it was thought, somewhat irreverently. The bent received by his mind in these early days will explain an occurrence which we shall afterwards have occasion to relate, in the language of a venerable Methodist Minister, still living. He seems however to have soon changed his mind with regard to a profession. He is found, shortly after his return home, acting as Prothonotary of the Supreme Court, and Clerk of the Peace for the District of Colchester. About the year 1800 he became a student in the office of Mr. Robie, then member for Truro, and afterwards Speaker of the Assembly. Two

years later, while still a student-at-law, he married Elizabeth Dickson, a daughter of Charles Dickson, Esq., then
recently deceased, who had been a member for Onslow,
while his own grand-father and father had respectively
represented Truro. Mr. Dickson had been a merchant
and shipbuilder, residing at Onslow, and doing business
on a large scale. He had a numerous family of sons and
daughters. Three of his sons were at a later date, at one
and the same time in the Assembly. With their brother
in-law, they made four members of one family, occupying
seats in that body. His marriage was followed by an
appointment to the office of Judge of Probate for the
Districts of Colchester and Pictou, which was conferred
upon him on the second day of July 1802.

He was admitted as Attorney and Barrister on the
6th April 1805, and from that day to the day of his death,
in 1846, his life was one of incessant activity. He sprang
into practice very rapidly, and, for over a third of a century, was a leading member of the profession.

In 1806, the year after his admission, he was elected
one of the members for the County of Halifax, which then
included, besides the County now known by that name,
the Districts constituting the Counties of Colchester and
Pictou. From 1806, when he entered the Assembly, till
1841, when he left it, he took a leading part in all the
public questions which arose during that long period. A
history of his life for that time is very much the history
of the Province. There were in the Assembly, during
this period, many able men, many eloquent speakers, and
powerful reasoners, but no one of them attained the dom-
inant and permanent influence which Mr. Archibald exercised over that body. No other man contributed so much
to mould the institutions and shape the destinies of Nova
Scotia.

CHAPTER II.

Politics in 1806. Sir. John Wentworth. William Cottnam Tonge elected Speaker and rejected. Mr. Wilkins becomes Speaker. Mr. Archibald's first motion in the Assembly. Takes charge of Road Questions. Religion in 1806. Kings College. Croke's Test Clauses. Controversy between two Bishops. Mr. McCulloch intervenes. He keeps a school. What followed.

The spirit in which the country was governed at the beginning of this century may be guaged, by a significant incident which occurred at the opening of the Session in 1806, the very day on which Mr. Archibald took his seat in the Assembly. Mr. John Wentworth was then Lieutenant Governor. He was a native of New Hampshire and had held the office of Governor in that Colony before the Revolution. He was also Surveyor General of His Majesty's Woods and Forests in North America.

Throughout the war Mr. Wentworth adhered steadily to the loyal side, and at the peace he removed to Nova Scotia, exercising the functions of Surveyor General over that part of the Continent which still remained subject to the King.

His services and sacrifices entitled him to the favorable consideration of the Crown. In 1792, he was appointed Lieutenant Governor of Nova Scotia, and some years afterwards was made a Baronet.

His experiences in the revolutionary contest had strongly tinged his political views. In his mind, liberal principles were merely a form of sedition or rebellion. Fourteen years experience in the Government of Nova Scotia had not moderated his prejudices. He was now over sixty four years of age, and any change, after that period of life, is not apt to be in the direction of increased liberality.

Sir John was now to meet the new House. It was summoned for the 18th November, 1806. On that day he came down to the Council Chamber, and sent for the Assembly. They attended and were, as usual, directed to retire to their own room, choose a speaker, and present him for approval. They did as they were bid, and presently returned with William Cottnam Tonge at their head, whom they presented in the usual form. Sir John, to their amazement, replied "I do not approve of the Speaker whom the House has chosen," and sent them back to their room with directions to choose some other member and present him for approval.

The gentleman so rejected, was eminently qualified for the position. He belonged to a family long connected with the Province. Winckworth Tonge, the father of Cottnam, was a Lieutenant in the 7th Regiment, or Royal Fusileers, and was on the Staff of the Duke of Kent, along with Brenton Halliburton, then Captain, and afterwards Chief Justice. For good service to his Sovereign under Lawrence and Moncton, former Governors, he had been rewarded by the position of Naval Officer, bestowed on him by the Imperial Government in 1773. He had owned a fine estate in the County of Hants, on which he had expended £3000, and upwards. He had been a member of the Assembly for over thirty years, and had been recommended by a late Governor to the Imperial Authorities as eminently qualified for a seat in the Council. On his death in 1792, William Cottnam Tonge, his son, succeeded to the estate. He was also appointed, by special mandamus from the Crown, to the position of Naval Officer, held by his father, and was returned by his father's constituency. William Cottnam was in no respect his father's inferior. He was well educated, able, eloquent and energetic, and soon made his influence felt in the Assembly, where he was found on all occasions, the advocate of liberal principles. His position, as a large landed proprietor, combined with his independent opinions, made him the natural head of the Country party, and a prominent opponent of the policy of the Governor and Council. Such was the influence, throughout the Province, acquired by his course in the Assembly, that when the election of 1799 took place, he was returned not only for Newport, where he had particular influence, but also came in at the head of the Poll for the County of Halifax, bringing with him as colleagues two country gentlemen, Mr. Mortimer of Pictou and Mr. Fulton of Colchester, who were of the same political sentiments with himself. This was the first breach in the monopoly of the representation of the Metropolitan county, which had hitherto been held by residents of the town of Halifax. It was further signalized by the defeat of Mr. Michael Wallace, a man of great influence and ability, who had held the county for twenty years, but who on this occasion, stood several hundred below Mr. Tonge on the Poll. So little had the influence of property to do with the result, that Mr. Tonge had not real estate in the county enough to qualify him as a member, and upon a petition he was unseated for Halifax and relegated to his return for Newport. Mr. Tonge had, in the last Session of the previous House, been elected and confirmed as Speaker, Mr. Uniacke being in England on leave of absence. Such was the man whom Sir John rejected as unfit for the office of Speaker. His feelings towards Mr. Tonge are shown in his official correspondence, with his Superiors in England. This is filled with statements and insinuations prejudicial to Mr. Tonge, and indicates intense dislike to that gentleman.

When Mr. Touge was presented a second time for for approval as Speaker it gave an opportunity which Sir John could not forego, to humiliate him and dismiss him with a mark of disgrace. The Assembly retired to their chamber, but do not appear to have been in any hurry to comply with Sir. John's directions. That day, and the next pass over, and nothing is done; but on the third day they proceed to business and select, and present, another gentleman who is duly approved. Thereupon Sir John delivers his speech which, of course, makes no allusion to the incident touching the Speakership. When however the House came to answer the speech they could not refrain from expressing in a short paragraph their feelings on the subject. They "lament the exercise by the Governor of a branch of the prerogative, long unused in Great Britain, and without precedent in the Province." Well might they speak of it as they did. The only precedent for the rejection of a Speaker, from the earliest ages, is older than the Revolution. There was indeed a curious coincidence between that case and the present. Charles the 2nd hated Sir Edward Seymour for much the same reason, and with much the same intensity, as Sir John Wentworth hated Cottnam Tonge, and both the English precedent, and the Nova Scotia precedent, would seem to have been prompted by the same motive; a desire on the part of the superior to humiliate and mortify a subordinate.

The temper of the House was probably affected by Sir John's contemptuous rejection of their choice. At all events, a few days afterwards, a curious entry appears on the Journals. On the ninth of December the Clerk informed the House that Mr. Wilkins, the new

Speaker, had been summoned to attend a meeting of the Governors of Kings College, and would not be able to be present till after the hour to which the House stood adjourned. A House, of course, could not be formed in the absence of the Speaker. They were *de facto* adjourned. Next day at ten o'clock the Speaker was in the chair. Mr. Archibald rose and offered two resolutions, the first he had moved since his entry into the Assembly. One of these resolutions, which was carried unanimously. asserted, that it was the first duty of the Speaker, and one to which every other duty should yield, to attend upon the House. The second, (on which there was a division) declared that a summons to the Speaker to attend any other duty at a time when the House was sitting, with notice so short as to prevent his consulting the House, was highly disrespectful to the Assembly, and that, if it was done again, it would be the duty of the Speaker not to attend, without the direction of the House. This resolution was carried by 18 to 12, after a debate of which we have no record. The proposition set out in the second resolution is so much a corollary from the first, that it is difficult to see how any one, not denying the major proposition, could controvert the minor. Be that as it may, the stand taken by Mr. Archibald on this occasion, shows his sense of the dignity of the House, and his determination to resist any infringement of its rights.

For the five years of that House, Mr. Archibald took a conspicuous part in shaping its business. His name appears more and more prominent as the time goes by. He seems early to have assumed, as his own special department, the division of the money for roads and bridges. This was probably due, in some measure, to

his long residence in the country, and his int'mate acquaintance with municipal business, one considerable part
of which is the improvement of the highways. All his
life, he considered the road service a most important
matter, and it was owing to his vigorous and steady exertions, that the leading roads from Halifax eastward
were so much improved. These formerly ran over the
crest of every hill, and were almost impassable by wheel-
ed carriages. Under Mr. Archibald's policy, they were
gradually altered to more level lines and put into travelling condition, till, in the times immediately preceding the
railroad era, the main road from Halifax to Pictou, which
was the thoroughfare to the East, was a pattern highway.

While a spirit so arbitrary in political matters as
that which distinguished the first act of the session of
1806 prevailed, a spirit equally intolerant was found in
matters of religion. The members of the Government,
with scarce an exception, belonged to the Episcopal
Church. That body had succeeded, in the first Session of
the General Assembly held in 1758 in obtaining an act of
the Legislature establishing their Church. A College was
afterwards erected at Windsor, and an act obtained in 1789
endowing it with £400, a year, out of the Provincial funds.
If the College had been open to all, this would have been
a praiseworthy appropriation of money; but unhappily
four fifths of the people of Nova Scotia were excluded
from its benefits, and insulted by its statutes. No pupil
was allowed " to attend Mass, or the Meeting Houses of
Presbyterians, Baptists or Methodists, or to be present at
seditious or rebellious meetings." It only wanted the
word " other" before the words " seditious or rebellious
meetings" to express the exact meaning of the framer of
the Statute, but even without it, the religious meetings of

several denominations of Christians, constituting four-fifths of the population of Nova Scotia, were in the same category with meetings for " sedition and rebellion." Is it to be wondered 'at that these bodies did not care to rally round an Institution, which their sons could not enter without abandoning the religious observances in which they had been trained? If indeed they could get over this obstacle, (and the experiment was tried in some cases) they had to go a step further before a degree could be obtained. It was not enough for a candidate to ignore his own creed. He was obliged to subscribe the thirty-nine Articles of the Church of England, in addition to three other articles passed by the Synod of London in 1603. What the latter may be, is not very well understood, but it is no great matter. Any Roman Catholic, Presbyterian, Baptist, or Methodist who could swallow thirty nine of the Articles would not likely strain at the other three.

Without due consideration of the political and religious atmosphere of the day, it would be impossible correctly to estimate the task that lay before the professors of liberal principles at the beginning of the Century. To be excluded from the highest social circles, to be branded as seditious or disloyal, to be subject to every impertinence and oppression which could be inflicted by men in authority, were only a part of the indignity and humiliation of those who spoke the words, or breathed the spirit, of free-born Englishmen. But intolerance, when extreme, always produces reaction, and reaction, was already beginning to show itself both in politics and religion. There was a small cloud in the horizon, not bigger than a mans hand, but it rose and spread till it covered the whole sky.

In tracing the history of the subject of our memoir

we are following the growth and expansion of liberal principles in their earlier stages. We have already spoken of the breach of the Halifax monopoly of representation made by Cottnam Tonge in 1799. In the election of 1806, the ground gained was not lost. Mr. Archibald came in for Colchester, and Mr. Mortimer was again returned for Pictou. The other two members were Mr. Robie, who had represented Truro in the previous session, and Mr. Lawson a Halifax merchant, a man of much liberality of sentiment. These four gentlemen formed the nucleus of a liberal party, which gradually grew more and more powerful in the Assembly.

At the same time there was another element at work, which contributed no small share to the growth of liberal feeling. About the time Mr. Archibald entered the Assembly, a controversy was going on between two prelates on the matters in difference between the Roman Catholic and the Protestant faith. Bishop Inglis, the first of that name, had written a treatise which called forth a reply from Bishop Bourke, who was a man of great ability, thoroughly conversant with his subject. The Roman Catholic Prelate was more than a match for his Protestant antagonist, and was begining to plume himself on victory, when suddenly there appeared a volume of some four hundred pages entitled "Popery Condemned by Scripture and the Fathers," which fell on the community like a clap of thunder. It was written with great ability, and displayed a wide knowledge of the writings of the early fathers. The wonder became greater, when it was discovered that the author of the volume was a poor Presbyterian Minister, preaching to a body of uneducated Highlanders, settlers on the shores of Pictou Harbour, who were just emerging from the bitterness of poverty through which they had been passing since first they had landed in the wilderness there, some twenty years before. The Rev. Mr. McColloch, afterwards well known as Doctor McCulloch, had, some five years before the appearance of his Book, arrived at Pictou in the Autumn of the year, on his way to Prince Edward Island, whither he was travelling, with a view to become Minister of a Congregation that had given him a call. The season, at the time of his arrival at Pictou, was so far advanced that he could not proceed further that fall, and this accidental detention in Nova Scotia during the winter caused a change of purpose, the effects of which will be long felt in this Province.

Mr. McCulloch's book was promptly met by a reply from Bishop Burke. This brought out as a rejoinder, "Popery again condemned", which gave still further assurance of the learning and ability of the poor Scotch Minister at Pictou Harbour. If he had not been poor, as well as learned and able, his detention at Pictou might not have affected so materially the future of the Province, but, driven to supplement by his own exertions, out of the pulpit, the scanty salary his people were able to pay him, he commenced teaching a school at Pictou. Gradually his views expanded, till he began to conceive the project of an educational institution for the youth of the dissenting bodies, and, if legislative aid could be procured out of the common fund for the College of one fifth of the population, surely there could be no objection, he thought, to a similar endowment to a College for the other four fifths.

In the popular branch the appeal was irresistible. Not so in the Council. There the battle was fought, year by year, for fifteen long years, and it was in this fight largely that the representative branch learned to appreciate its rights and privileges. Some members of the Council, themselves Churchmen, had the liberality to espouse the side of the people, and the sagacity to fore-see that the only way to calm the rising spirit, was to yield to it gracefully, before it acquired such violence and force as would not only attain the immediate object, but would sweep away in its current the power of the political body which obstructed its passage. Some of the best speeches in the Assembly for this long period, were on the subject of the Academy, the legislation on which was made to assume every variety of form, to meet the forces arrayed against it. Votes for its support were over and over again passed by the House, and rejected by the Council. Sometimes the vote passed the House unanimously and was still ignominiously rejected, till at length the Home Government had to interfere and administer a pointed rebuke to the Council, who at last yielded to fear, what they had refused to policy, and granted an endowment for ten years, under the dread, that unless they did so, a worse thing might befall them.

From the first appearance of this question before the Assembly, to the passage of the Bill which put an end to the agitation, Mr. Archibald took charge of the matter in the Assembly, and was the constant and unflinching friend of the Institution. The speeches he made upon it are almost innumerable, and, from beginning to end, he had the satisfaction of carrying with him on every occasion the great body of the representatives of the people. The discussions on this subject prepared the public mind for the stand afterwards taken by the Assembly in 1830, and paved the way for the still further changes in the constitution of the Country which followed the action of the House in 1837.

CHAPTER III.

1817 to 1825.

Mr. Archibald as an Advocate. King vs Sawers. King vs Holland. King vs Forrester.

We have treated the subject of the Pictou Academy without reference to chronological order. The final settlement of this question did not take place till 1831.

We shall now go back to a much earlier period and give some account of Mr. Archibald's professional work. His position in the Assembly seems not to have interfered, as it would in our days, with his practice at the Bar. He appears to have leaped at once into an extensive business, which he continued to hold, notwithstanding the demands upon his time exacted by Legislative and other duties. He had a large amount of office work, a class of business which a colonial lawyer always aims at, as the most lucrative branch of his profession. But his services were specially in demand on the trial of causes in Court. His name appears in almost every case of any importance reported, or referred to, in the Journals of the day.

After twelve years practice of his profession he was in 1817 appointed Kings Counsel. That office, at the time we are speaking of, was a mark of distinction. The Bar of the day consisted of thirty two members, while at the time of Mr. Archibald's appointment there was not a single Kings Counsel except the Attorney and Solicitor General.

In 1818 he acted as Surrogate General in the Admiralty, and gave Judgement in several cases then pending.

Some idea of the style of his forensic addresses may be formed from the reports of contemporaneous newspapers. These, to be sure, are meagre and imperfect; but enough may be gathered from them to show his skill in adapting his address to the case in hand, and to account in some measure for his great success with the Jury. We shall select as specimens a few of the cases in which he was engaged.

In 1819 he was retained for the defence in The King versus Sawers—an Indictment for assault and Battery. It was preferred by Dr. Hoffman against W. Q. Sawers, a well known lawyer, afterwards Judge of the Court of Common Pleas. The case originated in a quarrel between two respectable medical men, whose families are still represented in Halifax.

Dr. Hoffman was a German by birth, a native of Trieste. He was regularly educated for the profession, and had served in the British navy. He afterwards came to Halifax, where he married a Miss Mansfield, and settled down to the practice of his profession. His temper was somewhat uncertain, his knowledge of English very limited. It used to be said of him, that he had forgotten his mother tongue and never learned any other. His case against Sawers depended largely on his own testimony, which was given in a mixture of dialects that afforded much amusement to the bystanders.

Dr. Stirling was also a retired Surgeon of the Navy, by birth a Scotchman. He was well acquainted with his profession, a man of good general attainments and of respectable standing in society.

The quarrel began with a newspaper communication which was charged on Dr. Hoffman. It seems that on the day in question, there had been a conflict between the two Doctors in the streets, but they had been separated, and the assault by Sawers, now complained of, occurred later in the day. On Hoffman's examination, the defence naturally wished to get at the details of the first encounter, but the witness would not answer any questions on that point, and his refusal was sustained by the Court. The assault complained of was alleged to have been made by the defendant upon the Prosecutor, while he and Dr. Stirling were brandishing sticks at each other. The defence was that Mr. Sawers, seeing the two Doctors fighting, interfered to separate them and keep the peace.

When the case had been closed upon the part of the Crown, Mr. Archibald went to the Jury. After some preliminary observations he said "The Prosecutor had declined to give an account of what took place on the fifth November. He commmenced his narrative at one o'clock, when he states, he was informed that the defendant and Dr. Stirling had determined to attack him, but he would ask why had they determined to attack him, or why was Dr. Hoffman apprehensive of it? On this point the Jury would perceive, he declined to give any information. They would also perceive that when questions were pressed more closely, the prosecutor refused to answer. The reason is obvious, because it would have disclosed the transactions of the day; the real cause of all the evil that happened to him."

*　　*　　*　　*　　*　　*　　*　　*　　*

" From the evidence it appeared that the prosecutor was endeavouring to commit acts of violence against the defendant previous to the occurrence of the circumstances of which he complained. It was in his opinion necessary to relieve the minds of the Jury from the difficulty under which they must labor if no other evidence was offered them than what they had just heard. Could they imagine what induced the prosecutor to apprehend a breach of the peace on the part of Dr. Stirling? Was it merely that he saw him in the street and was afraid of venturing out? Were the Jury to consider the profession in this state of hostility to each other that one Doctor cannot safely venture upon the street if another is present? What in the absence of all evidence were they to conclude? Is it from the general peace of the world, that they were to conjecture the death of Mars without issue; and that his weapons and armour had, by some unknown law of inheritance, descended to the children of Esculapius? No, he would unfold to them the mystery."

The learned Counsel then proceeded to state the attack made by Dr. Hoffman upon Dr. Stirling a few hours before the present circumstances occurred, and painted in strong colors the impropriety of the conduct of the prosecutor, and of one Caliban, whom he styled his armour bearer, who had carried the whip with which the "prosecutor had attempted to chastise in the public street, a man not inferior to him in any point, either in education or respectability, in the community. He however was prevented, by the interference of persons who were present, and prudently retreated to the house of Mr. Mansfield, where the prosecutor stated he was called in his professional capacity to attend on one of the family. He however was satisfied that the prosecutor had not been attending in his professional line, as stated by him, but that he had commenced the day with a disposition to shed blood, and, having been foiled in his first attempt, he could not remain contented till he had stuck his lancet into one of the Mansfields." The Counsel then proceeded to state that Dr. Stirling had called upon Mr. Sawers in the meantime, and had informed him of what had taken place, and asked him to become his second, from which determination Mr. Sawers had dissuaded him, *and without any absence of honorable feeling,* prevailed on him to give up his intention. That Mr. Sawers afterwards saw Dr. Stirling, and the prosecutor engaged, and interfered to separate them. That in the act of so doing the injury happened of which the prosecutor complained. "In what way," he asked "were the contending parties to be put asunder? Was the defendant to interfere between them, by bowing like a young man of fashion, entering a ball-room; or by the force of his arms to separate them and place them at a distance from each other?"

 *   *   *   *   *   *   *   *   *

He next adverted to the words of the indictment which stated the prosecutor to be in the peace of God and our Lord the King, and after what had appeared "could the jury draw any conclusion that the prosecutor was cultivating those dispositions which descend from above and lead to the peace of mankind? Did it not rather seem that he was under the influence of those evil propensities which arise from the pit of darkness and overwhelm the children of disobedience?"

The prosecution ended in a verdict of not guilty which would seem to have been hardly justified by the facts given in evidence.

When Mr. Archibald, in the course of this address alluded to the proposition from which Mr. Sawers had dissuaded Dr. Stirling, and used the words '*without any absence of honorable feeling*', he gives a glimpse of the tone of sentiment on the subject of hostile meetings which prevailed in Halifax sixty years ago. Little did he then imagine, that before six months would pass over his head he would be called upon to vindicate the law of the land, in respect of a fatal event produced by the observance of this unwritten Code,—to prosecute a gentleman of his own profession, a friend and companion, a man of high principle and unimpeachable character, of elevated rank in society, the son of an Attorney General, himself at one time an Attorney General, but who in blind obedience to this law of Honor had accepted a challenge from a Mr. Bowie, a merchant of Halifax. The duel took place in the neighbourhood of what is now Richmond Station and Mr. Bowie fell. The surviving combatant was brought to trial, but fortunately for him, regard to the code of honor extended to every order of society, and was shared alike by Bench, by Bar and by Jury. Though acquitted, the accused felt the shadow of the sad event resting on him all through life.

We shall not dwell on the speech made by Mr. Archibald on this painful occasion, but rather hasten away to speak of another case, which gave an opportunity for the exercise of the lighter humour, in which the subject of our memoir preferred to indulge.

We refer to the case of " Ward versus Holland" which was a civil action for damages for an assault.

Mr. Robie appeared for the plaintiff, Mr. Archibald for the defendant.

Mr. Ward was the publisher of the Free-Press; Mr. Holland of the Recorder. Holland was stout and able, Ward puny and weak. Holland was a man of a reasonably good temper, but sometimes his Dutch blood got the better of him. Ward was habitually snarling and sarcastic. The two papers took opposite sides, and the publishers exchanged compliments very freely. At last the war became so hot that Holland threatened to cane Ward. The latter, hearing of the threat armed himself with a stick and prepared for defence. One day the parties met near the Scotch Church. In an instant Ward was down, with Holland's knee on his chest and his hand clutching his throat. Bystanders interfered, the victor was removed, and the prostrate man released. Forthwith Ward brought an action for the assault. The case was tried by a special Jury. It was easily proved. Indeed it would admit of no contradiction, and all that could be done, was to laugh it out of Court, if possible.

To understand one of the allusions in the Speech, it is necessary to premise, that Mr. Holland, who was a man of enterprise, had built a mill on the shore of the Basin, and was in the habit of manufacturing the paper he used for the Recorder.*

Mr. Archibald in addressing the Jury on the defence stated that he would call attention to the facts testified in the case, and also to the situation of the parties; when he was satisfied they would be of opinion with him that this cause was unworthy of the notice of a special jury. "Had this been a contest upon a Bill of Exchange or a policy of Insurance, the aid of a special jury would have been required—but it was neither. It was only a quarrel between two printers. Had there been any serious transgression of the liberty of the subject, or of the public peace, unprovoked, he would be as strenuous as any man to punish the aggressor; but, gentlemen, there are cases in which a jury will not visit a party transgressing the strict injunctions of the law with exemplary damages; if these are to operate to the benefit of him who first provoked, and would profit by, the transaction. He would call their attention to the situation of these parties. It

* Those who have to peruse the old files of that Journal will regret that Mr. Holland ever entered upon the Manufacturing business. The product is hardly fit for wrapping paper.

was but too well known they were printers and vendors
of news of all description—true and false—grave and
gay. In former times, two printers were sufficient for
this town; the King's printer informed us of all that
was to be known in the Government department, and
a chaste "Chronicle" recorded other events.—But the
age of novelty came and there arose an increased demand
for news and nonsense, which the correct men of the
olden times could by no means furnish. The consequence
was that other printers and other papers took the field.
The "Free Press" came last in hand, and was ushered into
the world after a learned prospectus which promised
everything that was chaste, learned or critical—in fact
everything except that which the paper had since contained. The very name of the learned Editors struck
terror into the other printers; and to finish the work,
unhappily for themselves, poor men! they made choice
of Mr. Edmund Ward as their printer. And from whence,
gentlemen, did he come? Have you not heard of his
exploits in Bermuda, of his correspondence with the Governor of that Island, where he kindled a flame which was
yet burning? They gave him there, gentlemen, a fair
trial—he was the King's printer, no less—but they at last
discovered exactly what he was—and had him shipped
off with all possible despatch. Here then, gentlemen,
he sat himself down, backed by the sagacious Editors of
the "Free Press"; and with the raging heat of a West
India climate upon him, he commenced attacking the RE-
CORDER. All competition in trade, as you know gentlemen,
is lawful, and Mr. Ward had a right in this most learned
paper (the like of which, as themselves affirmed, was not
to be found on this side of the Atlantic!" only think of
the range of country!) to contradict whatever was asser-

ted by the RECORDER. Finally the learned letters of
Agricola graced the pages of that paper, and the contradiction became doubly fierce. Agricola had his friends
who appeared as giants to Mr. Ward, and he fancied he
saw his ghost in one signature—his vision in another—
and his spectre in the ghastly grin of ANTHONY DOODLE-
DOO.* Did Agricola assert that the soil and climate of
Nova Scotia were adapted for cultivation : Mr. Ward and
his Editors labored to show that it was the seat of winter
and eternal barrenness. All this Mr. Ward had an undoubted right to do if he pleased; but, gentlemen, the
story ended not here. Mr. Holland, with a view of ben-
efiting the country and himself, erected a mill to grind
his paper; and while Mr. Ward was, every now and then,
apologizing to his subscribers for the want of that article,
and sending them a blue or brown sheet in place of a
white one, all that Mr. Holland required was a piece of
old junk, or a ball of spun yarn from the Dock Yard, to
furnish him for the work; and so well did he succeed,
that, at last, he could provide you with a history of the
coronation on the end of an old cable. This was really
too much for Mr. Ward, and he redoubled his attacks upon
our Agriculture, Anthony Holland, and the RECORDER.
At this time, the defendant, Philip Holland, my client,
who by the bye, is as quiet a man as ever lived—a sober,
cool-headed Nova Scotian Dutchman, began to be abused
by Mr. Ward. At one time he was represented as a mere
man of straw, a puppet in the hands of others—the wood-
en headed RECORDER man, and various other names equally
as *civil*, until Philip began to wax warm; but he bridled
his wrath, although with difficulty. At last Mr. Ward's
unlucky militant week arrived—young Agricola gave

* A writer in the Recorder over that signature, afterwards ascertained to be Mr. Archibald himself.

him a chastisement in the public square with a horsewhip, which he took very quietly, having brought upon himself. This sport, gentlemen, was of all things what he delighted in, and now was the time to bring out Philip Holland. Philip had already about as much as he could well bear; he was, in fact, like the cylinder of a steam engine, charged to the full height, when out came the last offensive paragraph—and he exploded. All his safety valves could not save him—and the dreadful explosion, in its full force, fell upon the head of poor Mr. Ward. Gentlemen, this *man of straw* raised his magic hand—and the printer of the " Free Press" fell prostrate before him, and, with him, all the high blown hopes of his learned Editors."

The learned counsel next proceeded to state that he was prepared, from the plaintiff's declaration and the statement of his counsel, to have heard a tremendous relation ; " but, gentlemen, so far as proof goes, Mr. Ward arose again with every drop of blood and every inch of skin he had when he fell ; whereas had Philip Holland been so disposed, he might have put his foot upon him, and extinguished him forever ! He was prepared to have heard that his body was as black as his types ; but such, gentlemen, has not been shown to have been the case ; he has not proved that there was either scar or scratch upon him ; and last of all he has had Mr. Holland fined in 40s. by a Justice, for the breach of the peace ; therefore all the mischief done to the public peace has been cured by the fine. Gentlemen, whom has Mr. Ward to blame for all this ? Most certainly himself. It is the man who seeks strife that finds it, and he would advise him to read the writings of Solomon in this particular, who was undoubtedly as wise as Mr. Ward and all his Editors together, and there he will find the infallible consequences of the line of conduct he has pursued. 'As certainly as the churning of milk bringeth forth butter, and the wringing of a nose bringeth forth blood, the forcing of wrath will bring forth strife.' Nothing but this kind of treatment would keep Mr. Ward in order. His old master and benefactor, Mr. Minns, as good a man as ever lived, this Mr. Ward insulted regularly every week in his paper.—He was the man who first taught him to set a type—and he was at last obliged to show him a cudgel to keep him quiet: he shook a stick over his head, and Mr. Ward has never troubled him since. The "Free Press" has observed ever since a prudent silence as to Mr. Minns and the "Weekly Chronicle." "Now, gentlemen," observed the learned counsel," "permit me to remark upon these parties (for I take both their papers) and have read the remarks of each upon the other; and very bitter they have been; but I have noticed that Mr. Ward has always begun and kept up the strife, and within the last three months he has let off several sneers at Mr. Holland, to which the RECORDER has paid no attention whatever. In their allusions to private character both parties were to blame, and were offensive to the community. Suppose, for instance, two persons whose aim was to set the town on fire, and who had been long attempting it, met by chance, measured fire brands with each other, and one of them got singed, should we who enjoy quiet, by reason of their encounter, complain and make this quarrel our case? No, gentlemen, leave them to finish it themselves, as they begun it. We have benefitted already by this beating; for both papers are more correct since the affair, and will become more guarded in what they publish. If Mr. Ward has anything to say to Mr. Holland, why does he not go to the office and say it to him manfully, instead of blazing it forth in his paper? No man likes to see his name abused in a public journal; and, for that very offence, Mr. Ward has often been threatened in this town, sometimes to be beat, sometimes to be horse-whipped, and sometimes to be skinned; but all would not avail; and if in this case you give him as much as will cover costs and charges, he will keep up the war, and no man will be safe. But, gentlemen, review his conduct. He wrote what he knew would bring him into trouble, and he armed himself with a stick for his defence, knowing the consequence of his writing, and will you give him damages such as are here demanded? No, gentlemen, give him one of the base copper coins now in circulation, for his damages, and another for his costs; and then you will give him as much as he deserves; and your verdict will in all likelihood be the means of restoring quiet to this community, by imposing a wholesome check on the language of Mr. Ward."

It appears by the Reporter's statement that the Court was convulsed with laughter during the delivery of this address. Judge Haliburton charged the jury, and as the assault was not denied, the jury were obliged to find a verdict for the plaintiff.

We now proceed to make some mention of a case of a different character from any we have noticed hitherto. It was tried in 1825, and it will show that, when occasion required it, Mr. Archibald could deal with a case in a very different style from that which distinguished the addresses we have quoted.

In April 1824, the ship Aurora left London with a cargo of goods for Halifax. The goods were worth from £20,000, to £30,000, and were fully insured. Some ten days after leaving port, the ship met with a terrible storm, and was so damaged as to be obliged to put back to Plymouth for repairs. The cargo was found to be damaged, but everything was done, that could be done, to prevent further injury, and the goods were repacked and sent on to Halifax. The cargo was consigned principally to the firm of S. Cunard & Co., but some portions of it were for other consignees. On the arrival of the vessel, the goods were examined, and being found to be damaged, a survey was held, and Messieurs Liddel, Mitchell and Russel were called upon to report on the condition of the cargo. By their advice, the goods were put up at auction and sold for the benefit of all concerned. DeBlois & Co., were the auctioneers. Shortly after this a letter signed ' James Cody' was received by the underwriters in London, representing that the writer was a person disposed to befriend those who were not on the spot to look after their own interests, and going into a variety of details, to show that the consignees, the auctioneers, and the Surveyors, were parties to a gross fraud, the object of which was, to buy in the goods for a price much below their value, and thus cheat the Insurance Office, to an extent sufficient to indemnify the importers for the loss they had sustained by the delay in the arrival of the ship.

Some gentlemen from Halifax having been in England that summer, enquiries were made of them to ascertain the standing of Mr. James Cody. Nobody knew a person of that name, and it was clear that there was no merchant of any standing in Halifax who bore it. This led to suspicion. The letter was sent out to the consignees for inquiry. They laid a trap to discover the writer, by mailing a letter addressed to Mr. James Cody and waiting till it should be called for. Eventually, one Little represented himself as ' James Cody', and asked for the letter,

which was delivered to him.   Next day he was arrested,
and then confessed that he had been sent for the letter
by a Mr. Forrester, who had opened and read it.   Thereupon Forrester, was indicted for libel, and, as a large
number of respectable men were assailed in the fictitious
letter, the trial naturally excited great interest.

Mr. Johnstone opened the case.   Mr. R. J. Uniacke
conducted the defence.   The case for the prosecution was
fully made out by the evidence.   Mr. Uniacke called some
testimony for the defence, when it became the duty of
Mr. Archibald to close for the Crown.

After commenting on the evidence which had been
adduced on the part of the defence, and showing a complete chain of testimony which proved the publication of
the libel, and traced its authorship to the defendant, Mr.
Archibald proceeded to deal with the criminality of the
publication.   "Upon this point" said he, " can there be a
doubt that a more base, defamatory, and malicious libel
was ever conceived in the imagination, or written by the
hand, of man?   All countries which bear any marks of
civilization, have a regard to character: and, in propor-
portion to the degree of civilization, is the value of
character estimated.   In our own happy country, that
reputation which arises from a conduct conformable to
the plain rules of common honesty, in our dealings with
man, is esteemed by every person of correct views, of
more importance to him than worldly wealth, inasmuch
as, without it, he cannot live respected, and worldly
wealth cannot purchase it for him ; but in addition to this
plain character of the humble man in society, there are
other characters all resting, it is true, upon the same base
of moral rectitude, but which, taken in connexion with
the standing of the individual, becomes of more import-

ance to him, and to the community of which he is a member."

"I might here" said the learned counsel, "enumerate many, but allow me to mention but one--that is—the character of a merchant. You," said he, "Gentlemen of the Jury, who are many of you merchants, know how well defined are all the requisites of such a character: and where is this character so highly valued as in that glorious country to which we belong? Now mark the conduct of the defendant. To the very metropolis of our country, the centre of commercial honour and commercial grandeur, was his poisonous slander directed, and at this very feeling point did it arrive. It was read among those merchants who conduct, upon the most honorable principles, the mercantile business of the world. What are the words and what the import of this abominable epistle? First, that the consignees of the cargo of the Aurora, themselves merchants, had, one and all, formed the base design, of making up a loss which each had sustained by the late arrival of this vessel, from the condemnation of her cargo, and when a sale should take place, the property should be purchased fraudulently by their agent, for their benefit; that the sale was advertised at 12, and took place at 10 o'clock, and that DeBlois the Auctioneer had previously agreed upon a private signal, by which the affairs of the sale were to be managed for the benefit of the assured.

I beg you to consider that not only those consignees are injured by the slander, but that the commercial credit of the Province is involved in it, and the interests of thousands perhaps affected by it. If it could be believed that these consignees, merchants, whose names were known as such in England, could lend themselves to

such a diabolical plot against the interests of their fellow
subjects and fellow merchants, who had insured their property, ought they not to be ranked among the most de-
graded of mankind? and their crime, for I will call it by
no other name, would reflect disgrace upon the whole
community of which they were members—yet this was
published and put forth, as true, where the persons injured had no opportunity of being heard, and where the
known and acknowledged uprightness of their conduct,
as it stands in this community, could not rise against it.
I come now to another part of this slander, aimed against
the persons who surveyed the damaged goods, John
Liddell, G. N. Russell and G. Mitchell. These gentlemen,
he states, were selected to answer the unjust views of the
consignees. As respects these gentlemen, would any man
dare, in the community in which they live, to utter an
expression against that irreproachable reputation which
they have so honestly gained, and which they so proudly
maintain? Yet has Mr. Forrester undertaken to represent them in no other way than as persons lending themselves to aid in one of the basest frauds which could be
practised against the interests of absent persons. But
mark how he has spoken of one of them. I mean Mr.
Liddell whom he has designated by his name of Office—
a magistrate—and you will see the intent of malice.
Among the changes of fortune which have attended the
fate of that gentleman, and which have reduced him, it is
true, from a state of comparative affluence, he has reason
to thank God, that he has maintained unshaken, the
character of an honest, independent man, one whom the
community intrusts with what concerns its best interests,
one who retains a reputation which the wealth of worlds
could not purchase for the being who has slandered him.

View therefore the production from beginning to end, and you must conclude that the framer of it was moved by the instigation of the Devil.

I cannot, Gentlemen of the Jury, conclude without calling your attention to one part of this case. It cannot pass unnoticed by me, and I am sure it cannot be so by you, or by their Lordships—I mean the assumption of the name of 'James Cody' by the defendant for the purpose of this slander. The God of nature, in His infinite wisdom, has so varied the human countenance that, among all the generations of men, there are distinguishing features for every individual, and from the same Author of our being, have we derived the authority and the precedent of giving to every individual his proper name, and this name when once solemnly assigned to the person cannot be changed, unless by the supreme authority of the Government—for no man's property would be safe, if names could be falsely usurped, and to personate another, is, by our law, in some cases, made a capital offence. The change of name is therefore considered the basest act of meanness. If in the words of the Defendant, ' a disposition to befriend those, who were not on the spot to see justice done to them, alone induced him to make the communication, why did he not come boldly forward in the face of day and say. "I Thomas Forrester have witnessed these misdoings and that is my name, and you know my place of habitation ;" but no, this would not accord with his intention. He was engaged in the hidden works of darkness and he wished to screen himself behind a shadow. Little did he suppose, when he was devising this wickedness privately, that it would be proclaimed this day, as it were, upon the housetops. Gentlemen in this case you are merely to say, Guilty or not Guilty. Were you called upon to assess damages I would ask you to compute them upon a scale that would leave the defendant like his friend James Cody, but a shadow and a name. Your task however ends with pronouncing him guilty, and I feel that you will say he is so, not in a slight degree, not merely tinged with guilt, but blackened to the core, and in this light must he appear in the eyes of every one who has any regard for the sacred value of character."

After a charge from Judge Halliburton who presided the Jury retired for about ten minutes and then returned with a verdict of guilty.

CHAPTER IV.

Interest in Agriculture. Manufacturing Operations. Visit to England. Appointed Chief Justice of P. E. I. Visits the Island. Address of Grand Inquest. Dinner at Pictou. Dinner and address at Truro. Made Solicitor General in place of Mr. Robie promoted. Chosen Speaker. Election of 1826. Again chosen Speaker. Non-residence in P. E. I. Aims at Chief Justiceship of N. S. Claims of different candidates. Changes impending. Grounds of Blowers' retention of office. Sir Peregrine Maitland's perplexities. Correspondence with Sir John Coape Sherbrooke. The misdirected letter.

We have grouped together in one connexion, these specimens of Mr. Archibald's forensic oratory, with a view to show the many sided character of his eloquence in addressing Juries. It will now be our duty to go back some years, to bring up our narrative in reference to matters unconnected with his professional pursuits.

In 1822 he undertook an enterprise, which was hardly to be expected from a person so engrossed as he was in professional and Parliamentary duties. He had ever since the appearance of the celebrated letters of John Young, published under the pseudonym of Agricola, taken a deep interest in the improvement of Agriculture in the Province. He was a member of the Halifax Agricultural Society, of which Mr. Young was Secretary, and was a regular attendant at its meetings. One of the main objects of this and kindred societies, established throughout the Province, was to promote the cultivation of cereal crops, and thus prevent the drain on our resources, arising from the importation of bread stuffs. With a view to encourage this kind of culture, the Legislature granted bounties for the erection of oat mills in the new settlements. In the older villages, mills for the grinding of

wheat were being erected, and Mr. Archibald showed
practically his sympathy with the movement, by erecting
at his own expense, a stand of mills at Truro.   These were
built in 1822, and so happily was the site chosen for
mechanical purposes, that from that day to this, manufacturing operations have been conducted on the spot.

In March, 1822, the University of Glasgow conferred
on Mr. Archibald, the degree of Doctor of Laws.

In 1824, Mr. Archibald spent some months in a visit
to England, and the continent of Europe.   While in England, he received marked attention from the Earl of Dalhousie, who was then Governor General of British North
America, but who had been, from 1816 to 1820, Governor
of Nova Scotia, and also from Sir James Kempt who was
then Governor.   Both these high officials were, like himself, on a visit to England on leave.   With Lord Dalhousie
Mr. Archibald had cordially co-operated in the effort
made by him to promote the improvement of agriculture,
and higher education, in the Province, two objects which
most deeply interested that nobleman, while here.   With
Sir James Kempt, Mr. Archibald was in entire sympathy
on a subject, which occupied much of the time and attention of that active and energetic Governor; the improvement of communications throughout the Province.   With
both these Governors, he was on terms of personal intimacy, and both had a very high opinion of his ability, and
social qualities.

The seals of the Colonial Office were held at the time
by Lord Bathurst.   He had been in office as Colonial
Minister ever since 1812, and was necessarily familiar
with the standing of the various Colonial statesmen of the
day.   The part which Mr. Archibald had taken in Provincial politics, naturally brought him into communication

with Lord Bathurst, who appreciated his merits and claims, and showed a desire to recognize them in any suitable way. There was at the time no public office vacant in Nova Scotia, which could be offered to him, but circumstances had occurred in Prince Edward Island, which rendered it desirable in the interests of that Colony, that some important changes should be made there. The Government of the Island was then administered by Mr. Smith, who had been appointed eleven years previously. During this long period many difficult questions had arisen; some of these springing from the peculiarity of the tenure of land in that Province. These questions required to be dealt with by an administrator of good temper and great tact, but unfortunately these were the precise qualities in which Mr. Smith was most deficient. He seems to have been irritable and arbitrary beyond the usual measure of the Governors of the day. He had succeeded in making bitter enemies of a large majority of the members of the Assembly, and of the other leading men throughout the Island. Finally he had given to his son-in-law, Mr. Lane, the appointment of Registrar in the Court of Chancery, and had incurred the ill will of the entire bar of the Island, by altering and adding to the scale of fees for that official. It was alleged, first, that the matter was wholly beyond his jurisdiction, and secondly, that the scale was so extravagant, that if the jurisdiction had been unquestioned, its exercise was indiscreet and injudicious. This seems to have been the culminating point of his misgovernment. The Bar as a body, memorialised Lord Bathurst on the subject, who had requested Sir James Kempt to name some suitable person to investigate the complaint. He had suggested Judge Halliburton for that service, and the Judge had been

charged to proceed to the Island to conduct the inquiry.
Meanwhile Sir James had arrived in London, where on the
sixth of July, he received and handed to the Colonial
Office Judge Halliburton's report. The conclusion at
which the Judge arrived is not within the scope of our
paper, for, without waiting for a Report, the Colonial Minister decided that Mr. Smith's administration had already
lasted too long, and accordingly in May, 1824, that officer
was superseded by the appointment of Colonel Ready to
the Government of the Island. But the Governorship
was not the only office that required a change. The Chief
Justice of the day was a Mr. Tremlet, who had been appointed about the same time with Mr. Smith. Mr. Tremlet was a man of fine social qualities, easy of temper, gen-
erous in manner, but a feeble and inefficient Judge. The
stronger will of the Governor dominated Mr. Tremlet's
gentler temper, and made the Judge a mere instrument
in the hands of Mr. Smith. The business of the Court
was greatly in arrear—the whole machinery of justice
disorganised. With such a Governor and such a Judge,
in a country where questions so difficult and intricate had
to be dealt with—the affairs of the Island were constantly disturbing the repose of the Colonial Minister. It was
necessary therefore to get rid, at once, of both Governor
and Judge. Sir James Kempt seems at the time to have
had the ear of the Colonial office on all matters connected with the Maritime Provinces. It was probably he
that suggested for the Chief Justiceship his friend, Mr.
Archibald, who in his judgment possessed precisely the
social and intellectual qualities, required for the office at
this juncture. The offer of the position was accordingly
made to that gentleman. He appears at first to have
hesitated about accepting it. At all events he would only

take it on the condition of being allowed to reside in
Nova Scotia, and follow his professional and political pursuits in that Province, going to the Island at such periods
as should be required for the due discharge of the judicial duties of the office. This condition being conceded,
he signified his acceptance, and was appointed Chief Justice by Royal Mandamus dated the 7th of August 1824.
No intimation of the appointment appears to have been
made for several months on either side of the Atlantic.
In the interval, the Colonial Office obtained the resignation of Mr. Tremlet. About the first of November, a
notice appears in the Halifax papers of a rumour that Mr.
Archibald had been appointed to the office in question.
On the tenth of November he arrived at Halifax, coming
by way of St. John, N.B. A few days afterwards he proceeded to the Island. On his way, he received an address
at Truro, from his old constituents, to which he made a
reply in his happiest vein. He was always on the footing
of warm friendship with the people of Colchester, and
never addressed them without giving expression to his
feelings toward them. On the twenty-first of November,
he reached Charlotte Town, and was duly sworn into office.
Colonel Ready had preceded him by a month. Both appointments appear to have given great satisfaction in the
Island. Mr. Archibald spent some three weeks at Charlotte Town, putting in order the business of the Court,
and then returned to Halifax. On his way, a public dinner was given him at Pictou, and another at Truro, at
both of which the usual number of pleasant things were
said of him, by his friends and constituents assembled to
meet him on these occasions.

The next session of the General Assembly began in
February 1825. Mr. Robie had been Speaker from the

time Mr. Wilkins was appointed to the Bench, eight years previously, till the second of April 1824, when he was elevated to the Council. The House was now therefore without a head, and when they met their choice fell unanimously on Mr. Archibald. Great changes had occurred in the Assembly since it was elected in 1820. As a consequence of the legislation of 1823, Mr. Marshall, of the County of Sydney, had gone to the office of First Justice of the Court of Common Pleas in Cape Breton. As a consequence of the legislation of 1824, Mr. Ritchie of Annapolis, and Mr. W. H. O. Haliburton of Hants, had left the Assembly for similar positions in the Middle and Western Districts of this Province, and now, the removal of Mr. Robie to the Council, took away the fourth leading member of the Assembly. Any House of thirty eight members, must have been a remarkable body, if it did not feel the depletion of its ranks by the absence of so many able men, and by the relegation to the quiet of the chair of a fifth man of Mr. Archibald's calibre.

The leading lawyers remaining on the floor of the House were Mr. Fairbanks of Halifax, and Mr. Uniacke of Cape Breton—the leading laymen, Messrs. Young of Sydney, Lawson of Halifax and Roach of Digby. The session of 1825 appears consequently not to have been very prolific in interesting discussions. After the rise of the House which sat for just two months, Mr. Archibald first attended to the legal business devolving upon him in Nova Scotia, and then proceeded to the Island, arriving in Charlotte Town in June. On the 2nd of July he was waited upon by the Grand Inquest of the Island, who presented him with an address of congratulation on his appointment, referring in very complimentry terms to the efficient discharge of his judicial duties which had already effected so much improvement in the Courts, and alluding to the charm of manner, which had already made him so many personal friends in the Island. The address concluded with the expression of a hope, that before long such arrangements would be made as would give them the benefit of his judicial services, and the advantages of his social influence, all the year round.

This was the first note of dissatisfaction with the condition of non-residence on which the Chief Justice had accepted the position.

In his reply he dexterously evaded the question, by general assurrances of his interest in the Island.

The Chief Justice continued about a fortnight longer, discharging his duties in the Court, and in the Executive Council, of which he was President. On the 20th of July he returned to Halifax. A few months later, he was appointed Solicitor General in place of Mr. Robie. That gentleman had received from the Crown a new office created on the application of the Governor. Sir James Kempt had complained to the Colonial Minister that much of his time was taken up by the duties incident to his office as Chancellor. That besides the loss of time, he felt his incompetency for the functions of a Judicial office without legal advice, and on his recommendation a new office was created by the Crown, that of the Master of the Rolls, to which Mr. Robie was appointed. This caused a vacancy in the office of Solicitor General to which Sir James nominated Mr. Archibald.

A general election took place in 1826. This brought into the House several new Members, who afterwards became men of considerable mark. Then first appeared in the Assembly Mr. Stewart of Cumberland, Mr. T. C. Haliburton of Annapolis, Mr. Murdoch of Halifax—all of

them men of more than average ability. No member of
any note in the old House, had disappeared from the
floor. The new material compensated in some measure
for the depletion of the previous three years·

When the House met in 1827, Mr. Archibald was
again unanimously chosen Speaker. The session commenced very quietly. The old members took a leading
part in the business, while the new men were becoming
acquainted with the rules of the House, and preparing themselves for the prominent part they were soon to play in
provincial politics. The duties of the chair kept the
Speaker off the floor, except on those occasions when the
House was in committee of the whole. There is consequently little record of speech or action on his part, during this and the following two sessions.

When next he went to the Island to do his judicial
work there, he found the feeling as to his non-residence,
of which the first note had been sounded in the address of
the Grand Inquest, was on the increase. This feeling was
natural under the circumstances. The more the people
valued and appreciated their Chief Justice, the more desirous they were that he should pass his time in the Island.
Besides it seemed derogatory to their position, that the
principal Judicial office in the Colony should be held by a
nonresident and be treated as an appendage to professional
and political pursuits in another Province. Mr. Archibald,
however, could hardly be expected willingly to confine his
ambition to the rewards offered by the Island. He was
not disposed to withdraw from the wider sphere, and the
brighter prospects, offered by his own country ; besides he
was bound to Nova Scotia, not only by the ties of interest
but by those of birth, and of strong personal attachment,
Here his professional practice was very large. He was

the head of the Assembly. He was also Solicitor General, while his superior, the Attorney, was an old man in feeble health. His accession to the higher office seemed to be an event of the immediate future. He appears to have early cherished the ambition to become Chief Justice of Nova Scotia. In this Province that office has always had a charm for our leading lawyers. Fifty years ago it was as eagerly sought after, as it was later on, when a race was run for many years between two prominent legal gentlemen, till the chances of politics assigned the prize to Sir. William Young.

Mr. Archibald held his Island office for over four years. At last, finding the dissatisfaction at his necessary absence increasing, and feeling moreover the burden of his other labors to be as much as he could well bear, he resigned the Chief Justiceship, and was succeeded by Mr. Jarvis on the 27th of October, 1828.

At this time the contending claimants for the chief position on the Bench of Nova Scotia were Judge Haliburton, Attorney General Uniacke, and Mr. Archibald. The Chief Justice of the day was Mr. Blowers, then at a very advanced age. He had been appointed to the office in 1797, and had therefore held the position for over thirty years. Of late he had not appeared in Court, or at all events had done so only on special occasions. The senior Judge was Mr. Brenton Halliburton, who had sat on the bench since 1807, and therefore had now twenty years of judicial experience. In the absence of the Chief Justice, he had presided over the Court, and for several years had done the duty of the Chief. The Attorney General, who in the usual course of events would have succeeded to the place of Mr. Blowers was, as we have already stated, an old man in infirm health. He had been appointed to his

present office on the same day as the Chief Justiceship
had been given to Mr. Blowers, and had therefore been
thirty years Attorney General.

It was clear from this state of things that considerable changes were at hand, and Mr. Archibald cannot be
blamed if he used his best exertions to attain the coveted
prize.   Mr. Uniacke's age was against him in the competition.   The contest, therefore, lay between the senior Puisne
Judge, and the Solicitor General.   Each of these had considerable claims—Mr. Halliburton had now a long experience on the bench.   The infirmities of his Chief had
thrown upon him many of the duties belonging to his
superior in office.   No training could better fit a person
for the position of Chief Justice.   Besides, he was an able
lawyer, and an excellent man, dignified in manners, plea-
sent and genial in social life, and a favorite in the community.   He was also a Member of the Council, and connected by family ties with other leading members of that
Body, and could control its influence, so powerful at the
time we are speaking of.   But on the other hand it was
said, that if he had had the experience, he had also been
in receipt of the salary, of a Judge during that long
period.   He had stepped into office without any of the
toil or sacrifices which generally precede valuable appointments.   He had been in early life in the Army, and while
the Duke of Kent remained in Halifax, he had been
attached to his staff, and had enjoyed all the pleasures of
a Court life, and all the comforts of an officer's pay.   When
the Duke left Nova Scotia, Mr. Halliburton resumed the
study of law, which he had abandoned for arms.   He was
admitted in July, 1813, and in a little over three years
from that date was appointed to the Bench.   He had never
represented a constituency, he had had none of the labors

or toils by which a public man earns his right to official
appointments. True it is, that after the lapse of thirteen
years, he became a member of His Majesty's Council, but
with the toil of that office, he possessed also its power
and patronage.

On the other hand, Mr. Archibald had been in the
Assembly almost as long as Mr. Halliburton had been on
the Bench—he had taken an active part in every question
that came before that body since he first became a member. He had run five elections, which were not held on
one day, as now, and which, as then conducted, involved
much toil and expense. He had worked his way by
talent and merit, and without patronage or friends, high up
in his profession. He had exercised the large influence
he possessed in the Assembly, and in the country, in the
interests of good government, and, holding as he did, to the
Attorney General of the day, a relation much like that
of Mr. Halliburton to the Chief Justice, he might fairly
consider himself entitled to the position always claimed
by the holder of the Attorney General's office in Nova
Scotia, on a vacancy occuring during his incumbency.

With such an equality of claim, it was evident that
the struggle for the position would be keen, and, at the
advanced age of Mr. Blowers, it was equally evident that
the crisis was not far off.

It is said that the Chief Justice had long been willing
to resign, if he could be sure of Judge Halliburton suc-
ceeding to his place, but he did not like Mr. Uniacke, the
Attorney General, whose claim he supposed would be
successful. Mr. Blowers was of Colonial, Mr. Uniacke of
Irish, extraction. Blowers was a man of medium stature,
of refined taste, scholarly in tone of mind, gentle and
kindly in manner. Uniacke was of figure, tall and thin,

rough and brusque in manner, without much scholarship,
but possessing considerable parts and great humour.   He
affected the brogue on all occasions when it suited his
purpose.   No two men could be more unlike each other
than Blowers and Uniacke—and, so long as there was
danger of the Chief-Justiceship falling, in case of vacancy,
to Attorney General Uniacke, Mr. Blowers would have
considered it his duty to hold on to it.   It does not appear
that Mr. Archibald's aspirations for the office were known
at the time.   Mr. Halliburton even appears not to have
suspected that Mr. Archibald was a competitor.   The
Attorney General was evidently the "bête noire"
both with the Chief and the senior Puisne Judge.   A
curious despatch of Sir Peregrine Maitland throws some
light on the contest.   When Sir James left here in August
1828, to assume the Government of Canada, he was succeeded in Nova Scotia by Sir Peregrine Maitland, who did not
however arrive here till November following.   Shortly
afterwards he asked and obtained leave to go to Barbadoes
for his health.   On reaching that Island, he found it in a
bad sanitary condition.   He then came to Bermuda, from
which he addressed a letter to Sir George Murray, then
Colonial Secretary, which gives some glimpses of the state
of things as between the rival candidates for the falling
Chief Justiceship.   It seems that the Attorney General
had previously forwarded to the Colonial Office a statement of his claims, but since that time a new Chief had
succeeded to that department, and Mr. Uniacke appears
to have been apprehensive that his papers would be over-
looked.   He had therefore enclosed a new set to Sir
Peregrine at Bermuda, to be forwarded by him to the
Colonial office.   It seems also that Sir Peregrine had
sometime before this transmitted to the same office a

Memorial from Mr. Archibald, the Solicitor General and Speaker, bringing his services to the notice of the Crown, and had accompanied the papers by a letter of his own, "making such favorable mention of that gentleman as his conduct appeared to merit." He had also recently received a letter from Judge Halliburton, who seems, all of a sudden, to have discovered that Mr. Archibald was on the same track with himself. A flood of correspondence is thus suddenly poured in upon Sir Peregrine and the Colonial Office. In Sir Peregrine's letter to the Minister, after all this had occurred, he says, among other things, that " when he wrote before about Mr. Archibald's services, it did not occur to him that that gentleman was looking for the Chief Justiceship, but being informed by Judge Halliburton that he was certainly aiming at that office, he had therefore thought it but fair to transmit Judge Halliburton's Memorial, and at the same time to make Mr. Uniacke, the Attorney General, a long tried and faithful servant of the Crown, acquainted with the steps he had taken, as, from the usual course which he believed the line of preferment had taken in the Colony, he supposed Mr. Uniacke would feel interested in the subject." He goes on to apologise for a correspondence, which he could not but consider premature, inasmuch as it related to the filling of a vacancy, before there was a vacancy to fill.

The discovery of Mr. Archibald's aspirations, for the Chief Justiceship, seems to have been made after the House met in 1829, and steps were taken to get at the truth, which savor strongly of the habits of that day. The incidents connected with the discovery, are detailed at large in a communication sent sometime afterwards to the *Free Press*, written from the standpoint of the Council,

and in opposition to the pretensions of the Speaker. It
would seem from this article that when suspicions arose
as to Mr. Archibald's candidature, the other parties set
themselves in motion. The Judge and the Attorney General were prepared to contest the matter between themselves, but they were indignant at the presumption of the
third candidate. He was not a member of the Council,
and yet he ventured to aspire to such an office. They
called on him and charged him with "endeavouring to
use undue influence with His Majesty's Ministers to get
himself appointed Chief Justice of the Province, when
they as the Attorney General of the Province, and the
Judge of His Majesty's Supreme Court, were as eligible
from their offices, and as much entitled from their services to the situation, when it became vacant, as he
could possibly be from any similar consideration." The
writer goes on to say that the interview was not very
satisfactory to the parties who had sought it, that Mr.
Archibald treated them both with scant courtesy, and
gave them no explanations. Shortly afterwards the
Judge and the Attorney General, in conjunction with a
third gentleman (whose name is not given) wrote a letter
to Sir John Coape Sherbrooke, requesting him to call at
the Colonial Office, and ascertain the facts relative to Mr.
Archibald's correspondence, at the same time requesting
his co-operation in laying their claims before Sir George
Murray, for the consideration of His Majesty's Ministers."

These incidents are all stated as 'from the best
authority.' They are made the basis of charges against
Mr. Archibald, which we shall have occasion to examine
by-and-by. As to the facts, we may take them as stated.
The charges are entirely matter of inference. We are in
as good a position as the writer to make any deductions
warranted by the facts.

Poor Sir Peregrine, in Bermuda, must have felt very uncomfortable in having to play the part of second to each of the three candidates, in this curious tri-angular duel. All parties consulted him, and all parties distrusted him, and thenceforth carried on their negotiations directly with the Colonial Office.

The letter which Sir Peregrine Maitland wrote from Bermuda, from which we have already quoted, was the result of a communication he received from Judge Halliburton, on the discovery already referred to being made.

When the Judge and Attorney General despatched the letter to Sir John Coape Sherbrooke, they had little anticipation of the curious sequel which was to occur. Sir John it seems made his application in due course at the Colonial office, and obtained the information sought for. This he forwarded, as he supposed, to the gentleman who had written him. But unluckily he had very hazy recollections of the Provincial dignitaries with whom he had been associated while Governor of Nova Scotia. Indeed Sir John was now very ill, and died shortly afterwards. In his state of health, he blundered in the address of his letter in reply. He directed it to the Solicitor instead of the Attorney General, and thus information of the whole proceedings was given, by the friend of the Judge and Attorney General, to the very person from whom they would have been most anxious to withhold it.

When we come to resume our narrative at this point, we shall find the scene of action transferred to the other side of the water. There indeed it will be found that Mr. Uniacke, one of the candidates, was unable to appear in consequence of failing health, which terminated in his death before the vacancy occurred. This circumstance reduced the number of the combatants to two, and took away the triangular feature of the contest. But before we relate the result, we shall have to bring up the thread of our narrative on other matters to that date.

CHAPTER V.

The year 1830 was a remarkable epoch in the history of Nova Scotia. The Assembly comprised a number of gentlemen who would have done honor to the Legislature of any country. Among the lawyers, to pass by Mr. Archibald, for the present, there was Fairbanks of Halifax, a man of great force of character, well versed in commercial law, and concerned in every important case before the Courts in which the principles of the "lex mercatoria" were involved. If not eloquent, he was at all events, a powerful and persuasive reasoner, and had taken a prominent part in all the discussions in Parliament since he succeeded to the seat for the Town of Halifax, vacated by the death of Mr. Grassie.

There was Stewart of Cumberland, who had entered the Assembly in 1827, and whose name appears in the Journals from that time on, as one of the most active members of the House. He was remarkable for the torrent of impetuous eloquence which flowed from him, and for the power of sarcasm with which he could overwhelm an adversary. There was Richard J. Uniacke the younger, a man of more than average ability, and like all the Uniackes, possessed of great command of language. He fought the battle of the Council and of his father with great energy and vigor. There was Murdoch, the colleague of Fairbanks, then comparatively a young man, who, during the debates of this Session, displayed high powers of mind, and gave assurance of qualities which

would have made him eminent as a politician. Fortunately for Nova Scotia, if not for himself, a hasty speech,
made at the hustings at the following general election on
nomination day, offended some of his constituents, and reserved him for service as an historical pioneer. We need
not mention Thomas Dickson, of Pictou, who represented
Sydney County, or Morse, of Amherst, both of whom
were men of more than ordinary ability.

Among the laymen, were a number of men of sound
judgement and great weight of character; but towering
far above the ordinary level, was one whose *nom de plume*
of 'Agricola' was even better known perhaps throughout
Nova Scotia, than that which he bore in ordinary life.
Mr. Young, among the galaxy of professional men who
surrounded him, was always ready to take his part in
any discussion, and to sustain it by clear and lucid oratory, which no other man of his day possessed in equal
perfection.

In fact it may be said with truth, that since the days
when the House drew its members from the men of culture and ability, who were educated in older countries,
and who took up their abode here at the close of the Revolutionary War, with the single exception of that of
1820, no Assembly possessed so many men of mark as the
one of which we are speaking. Any gentleman who
could assume and retain the position of leader in such a
body, must have been a man of no ordinary character.

The speeches which, in the course of our narrative
we shall have occasion to quote cannot well be understood, or the allusions in them appreciated, without some
explanations about the matter in controversy.

The Legislature met on the eleventh of February
1830. Sir Peregrine Maitland was then in Bermuda on

a nine months leave of absence. Mr. Wallace the Treasurer, as next senior member of Council after the Chief Justice and Bishop, who were excluded by the Royal instructions, administered the Government. The session began very quietly. There were no exciting questions before the country. In his opening speech Mr. Wallace said he had nothing to communicate to the House from the Colonial Secretary. He recommended harmony in the proceedings, and as much expedition as was consistent with the nature of the business to be brought before them.

Never had a session opened with less appearance of a storm. Mr. Wallace was an old and favorite public servant. Sir Peregrine Maitland had last year recommended the Imperial Government as a reward of his long and faithful public services, to confer the office he held, upon his son Charles. Nothing however had been done. Shortly after the Legislature met at this session, an address to His Majesty passed the House, and another the Council, praying that the appointment should be made as recommended by Sir. Peregrine. The President was therefore on the best of terms with every branch of the Legislature. There was some inconsistency in his administering the Government and at the same time ho'ding the office of Treasurer. This seems to have struck Mr. Blowers the Chief Justice, who called attention to it at a meeting of the council in its executive capacity, held just after the departure of Sir. Peregrine. Mr. Wallace then stated that he had appointed his son to do the duty, and that his own bonds remained still in force. The explanation did not do much to clear up the difficulty, but it satisfied a friendly Council. All went smoothly till one of the revenue bills, the one which levied a duty on

Spirituous Liquors, came before the Council. One of the clauses imposed a tax of one shilling and four pence a gallon on brandy. An act had been passed in 1826, and every year thereafter, which was supposed to charge brandy with duty to that amount. That sum was collected at first, but afterwards, by some curious construction of the officials, only one shilling a gallon was exacted. The extra fourpence paid for some time was returned to the importers from whom it had been collected. This fact did not come to light till after the session opened. Messrs. E. Collins & Co. (the senior partner being a member of Council) presented a petition to the House, claiming compensation for the loss sustained in paying liquor duties in Doubloons, below their fair value. The investigation which followed led to the discovery by the House that the law had been evaded. Naturally enough they were indignant. They found the firm, which should have paid one shilling and fourpence and had been let off at one shilling, striving to take still more out of the Treasury, and the fact that Mr. Collins, a member of the Council, was a party both to the evasion and to the petition, increased their disgust. They were resolved therefore that the new act should express their meaning in words that could not be misunderstood, and they framed their measure accordingly.

The fourpence which constituted the ground of difference was calculated to yield about £700. With such a revenue as the Province had at the time, under its own Revenue Acts, the difference between 1s. and 1s. 4d. would be less than an addition of one eighth of one per cent to a ten per cent tariff. It was a matter of perfect insignificance. When the Bill went up to the Council on the 29th March, that body demanded a conference. The House acceded.

At the conference the Council objected to the extra four-pence as " a burden upon commerce greater than commerce could bear." The members from the Assembly adhered to their Bill, the members from the Council to their objection. The conference broke up, and its members reported to the respective Houses. On the 31st March another conference was demanded by the Council, which was held, but without effecting any change of opinion in either body. At an early hour of the afternoon of that day, the Council sent down all the other revenue bills duly agreed to. Sir Peregrine came down to the Council Chamber and gave his assent. At a still later hour, about four o'clock P. M., the Council sent down the Bill in question, with a message that they did not agree to it. What was to be done ? As the Revenue Acts were then framed, they expired on the 31st March, at midnight. It was within a few hours of that time. The warehouses were full of Spirituous liquors, which could be thrown on the market without payment of duty immediately after twelve o'clock P. M. The loss to the Revenue might be computed at £40,000. The House never supposed that the Council would take the extreme measure of throwing away the Revenue on all spirits, to gain an exemption of fourpence on brandy. No wonder that there was great excitement. No body was prepared to suggest a course of action. Nothing was done that evening, but next day, at the opening of the House, Mr. Stewart introduced a new Bill, to revive the Act that had just expired. It passed the same day through all its stages and on Tuesday was sent to the Council. There it remained till Saturday when it was returned to the House disagreed to, with a memorandum explaining the cause of its rejection. The old statement that ' the burden was greater than commerce could bear' was still adhered to, but the bill was rejected on the further ground that the Council had already passed upon a Bill with the same provisions, and that it was against parliamentary rules, to send up the second time in the same session, a bill already disposed of.

In reality the Bill was different, not in title only, but in its provision, which was to revive a bill that had expired, and also in the period of time covered by it, which was necessarily different from that in the former bill. Thus it was that the true interests of the Province were sacrificed to a technical objection, which was itself unfounded. Meanwhile a committee that had just been appointed to search the Journals of the Council in reference to the proceedings on the first bill, reported that at its second reading in Council it had been referred to a Committee consisting of the two collectors and Mr. Collins the head of the firm of importers whose petition had lately been before them, and that it was on the report of these gentlemen that the bill had been rejected, and further that the rejection of the Bill took place, before the last conference was held to which the House had been invited. The discovery of the evasion of duty by the importers, and its sanction by the collectors, added to the indignity of amusing the House with the pretence of a conference on a matter which the Council had already disposed of, occasioned much of the bitterness which marks the speeches subsequently made in the Assembly. Up to this time Mr. Archibald had taken little part in the proceedings. His position in the chair precluded him from addressing the House except when it was in Committee of the whole. And hitherto their had been no occasion for his active interference.

When Mr. Stewarts bill went into committee of the whole House, the question as to the amount of tax was raised. Mr. Lawson proposed that the blank in the bill for duty on brandy per gallon should be filled up with one shilling and fourpence. Then began a discussion in which Mr. Archibald took a prominent part.

Mr. Dill was the first speaker; after him came one or two other members, but the subject was approached with much hesitation.—Many were uncertain, whether after all it would not be best to yield the point. Nobody was anxious to take the floor. Mr. Young, who was among the first to speak, commenced his address by noticing the hesitation which was prevailing. Mr. Young was a corpulent man. He said that he seldom had an opportunity of speaking early in debates, in consequence of gentlemen of much lighter bodily weight being sure to rise before him, but he found no difficulty on this occasion. He said that while they were deliberating the merchants on the outside were acting, and at that hour upwards of £1100 worth of dutiable articles had been thrown on the market without paying duty. He sustained the tax of one shilling and fourpence in an able and well reasoned speech. Several other members followed. Mr. Dill, member for Windsor made some observations which brought him into great prominence a few days afterwards. He " declared that he did not like to make reflections, but he thought that it was rather singular that one gentleman connected with His Majesty's Council was himself interested in a large quantity of brandy, and that availing himself of the state of affairs that he had assisted to bring on, he had endeavoured to evade the duty, and notwithstanding the raging of the elements," (for it appears there was a frightful storm on that day) " he had caused it all to be removed from the warehouse."

Other members followed, but the debate languished and the chairman was about to put the vote, when Mr. Archibald rose and delivered the first of a series of splendid orations upon the subject matter of the dispute between the two Houses. The debates in the House were not then reported with much accuracy, but enough is to be found in the columns of the different newspapers of the day, to afford the means of judging, somewhat of the character and style; and very precisely of the effect of the addresses delivered.

Mr. Archibald said he hoped the Chairman would not put the question immediately, it was a subject of too much importance to be decided hastily, and he wished gentlemen to pause and consider well before they came to a determination. The House on a former day had had the subject of a supply before them, and after mature deliberation, came to the conclusion to pass the Revenue Bills in the shape they had been sent to his Majesty's Council. It was certainly the undoubted privilege of this House to determine what amount of Revenue should be raised from the people of this Province; and to fix and establish the rate of duty to be imposed on each particular article. This right the House had constitutionally exercised: and upon what ground, he would ask, was it that His Majesty's Council had rejected the supply, which they, the representatives of the people, had so liberally tendered to the representative of His Majesty? Much had been said about the stand made by the House in the conference with His Majesty's Council, but he could not see how this House could with propriety have conducted that conference otherwise than they had done. He called the attention of the House to the Acts which passed in 1826. In that year the revenue laws of this Province underwent a thorough revision, and, after much discussion and mature deliberation, a system of finance was adopted, which had been continued without material alteration to the present time. By the law of that year, which the House had this year re-enacted, the article of foreign brandy was intended to be subjected to a provincial duty of one shilling and fourpence a gallon, and the members of the House had ever believed that that duty had been regularly collected. Our committee appointed to investigate the public accounts, discovered that there was a deficiency in the revenue for the last three or four years, according to their reading of the Act, of nearly £3000., and they were about to report that the collector of Impost and Excise be surcharged with the amount of these duties. The petition of Messrs. Collins & Co., praying for a return of part of the duties levied at the Custom House on foreign brandy, drew the attention of the House particularly to this subject, and then for the first time it was discovered that the additional fourpence which the act of 1826 intended to impose, had not been collected.

* * * * * * * * *

Mr. Chairman, (continued the learned Speaker.) It is in vain for us to sit here if it be not to maintain the rights of the people whom we represent:—and it is in vain for us to attempt to maintain their rights, if we do not preserve the privileges, which belong to their representatives. If when we are asked by His Majesty to grant a supply, and if when we have liberally provided for the Public Service, the Revenue Bills are to be thrown back upon us in this way, and at this time, we may as well resign into the hands of our constituents the faint semblance of a power to grant supplies, and apportion their burdens, which in reality we do not possess. When Sir it is said that the Revenue bills were not sent to His Majesty's Council until a late period in the Session, let me remind gentlemen of the time the large appropriations for the road service lay before that Honorable Body; after the principal sum had been agreed to, the specific appropriations had remained there for fifteen or twenty days, and then came down to us rejected: and it was not until the House had to resort to measures to which I most unwillingly submitted that this highly important service was secured. Was it to be expected under these circumstances, that this House should part with its own main constitutional check upon the other branch of the Legislature; and that Revenue bills should be sent to His Majesty's Council whilst the House remained in doubt whether any appropriation would be made of the money already in the Treasury? But Sir, these Bills were sent to the Council early on Monday last, and there was abundance of time to consider them. They were in form and substance the same bills which have been passed for the last four years: the only alteration being the addition of fourpence upon British spirits, which fixed the duty on foreign brandy at the rate intended by the Legislature when the original Bill passed in 1825, a duty which it can well bear. But let us see what was the course pursued by his Majesty's Council with this bill. The Committee of this House appointed to search their Journals, have reported their proceedings. I find that this Bill was referred to a Committee of that Honorable Board, and of whom, let me ask, did the Committee consist? The Collector of His Majesty's Customs, the Collector of Impost and Excise, and Mr. Collins, a merchant extensively engaged in that trade which is most affected by this Bill. Mr. Chairman

I deal in no personalities, nor will I use disgraceful language. His Majesty's Council have a right to constitute any part of their Board, a committee for any particular purpose. But what were this Committee to do? Were they to report upon the regulating clause of the Bill, to see that no foreign matter was introduced, or that no favorite measure of this House was tacked to it? No, Sir! they were to report, it must be presumed, whether or not in the opinion of those two officers, the servants of the province, and to whom heavy and burthensome salaries are paid for collecting its revenues, and in the opinion of the Honorable gentleman so deeply interested in the trade, the representatives of the people had exercised a correct judgement in imposing upon their constituents the taxes they were to pay for the public service of the country—and even for payment of the salaries of two of the Committee, who were thus to report upon the proceedings of the Assembly. The Committee of this House in conference were distinctly informed, that His Majesty's Council are of opinion that the duties on all the various articles enumerated in the Bill are too high. Not contented with this general declaration they descend to particulars—the duty on brandy should be 20cts. on rum 10cts., on low wines 1s. 3d, and so on upon all the various articles: and having made this important communication, they dismiss our Committee with a written tariff to report to this House the sage suggestions of His Majesty's Council. Sir. long as I have had a seat in this Assembly, this is the first time His Majesty's Council have ever presumed to dictate to this House the principal duty to be imposed upon any article of consumption. This encroachment upon the privileges of the people, this attempt to point out the course we are

to pursue in raising a revenue, is a new lesson of degreda-
tion to be taught the Representatives of Nova Scotia, and
it is one which I trust they will not be apt to learn. But
why was the duty too high? what reason existed in the
mind of this Honourable Committee and the Board for
reducing the duties at this time? Is it not the period of
all others, when the spirit of improvement is in full exercise? Are not out roads and bridges, our schools and our
public works, our agriculture, our fisheries and our commerce all dependent upon the revenue, and have we not
in this session appropriated large sums to these various
services? Have we not also a heavy debt on which we are
paying interest, and that too to some of the salaried men
of the Province, who perchance hold a seat in His
Majesty's Council, and now forsooth would diminish our
means? Is this a time then, and are these the circumstances, under which His Majesty's Council would dictate
the reduction of our revenue, and compel us to the measure? Although we feel in no small degree the pressure
of commercial embarrassment, we are able and willing,
I say, Sir, we, the people who are represented in this
House, are all able and willing to raise sufficient sums for
the public services of the country. It is the undoubted
privilege of the House to impose all burthens to be borne
by the people, to originate and to frame all money bills,
and it is we, and we alone, who are to determine what
article can best bear a duty, and what classes of men are
most able, from the consumption of dutiable articles, to
contribute to the Revenue of the Country. This privilege
is the most important right which the Commons enjoy.
His Majesty's Council cannot add to or take from the
duties we impose; and if we should suffer an encroachment upon this prerogative,—if we allow this privilege

to be wrested from us, while we are thus exercising it with discretion, there will be an end of the influence of the people in the Legislature, and we may quietly resign to His Majesty's Council the full and uncontrolled power of raising the Revenue, and of appropriating it, if they see fit, without the rude interference of the House of Assembly.

His Honor the President in behalf of His Majesty requests this House to grant the usual supplies for the public service, and when these supplies are liberally granted, the Council standing between His Majesty's representative and the grant made him, throw it back upon the representatives of the people. And in point of time when is this done? On the last day of the operation of the former law, and within eight hours of the midnight which terminated its existence. Now Sir, with all the conferences that have been had, what could the House have done on that day more than was done? I had not an opportunity of offering an opinion. I was in that chair and felt myself only bound to keep the order of the House without any desire to influence its decision. The House came to the determination to make no change, and how could they determine otherwise? The Bill had finally passed the House, and was before the council. Surely they could not expect us to alter or amend a money bill! and how indeed could this House consider the matter of a bill which had passed out of their possession, and was then before another branch of the Legislature? Was it expected that the dictation of the Committee of Council, or the threat that they would not agree to the bill unless the fourpence was relinquished, was to terrify us to submit to an encroachment upon our privileges or accede to an unconstitutional proposition, which the House of Peers, the ancient hereditary Baronage of England would never have presumed to make to the Commons? Gentlemen have said that the last conference ought not to have been asked—that the instructions given to our Committee had influenced the determination of the Council on the bill. But turn to the extract from the Council Journals, and we find that before this conference was held, and before the Council had agreed to the last conference with the House, the bill had met its death blow. It had been rejected, and the Deputy Clerk had been ordered to carry it to the House with that message. The retaining the bill and agreeing to conference, after it had been disagreed to, was merely giving color.

The mischiefs of this measure were not easily to be calculated. In a moment all is thrown into confusion, and in every part of the Province the same scenes will be acting.

The warehouses are thrown open, and dutiable articles are in the act of being transported to every part of the town and country without payment of duty. But it is not merely the amount of revenue that is lost, and the consequent embarrassments of public credit : but mark the injury to the merchant who has imported largely, and paid or secured his duties, and now finds a deluge of the same article poured into the market without any charge upon it! This House, no doubt at a future day, will be assailed from all quarters with grievances arising out of this transaction, which they cannot redress. Mischiefs will follow in the train of this rejection round the whole of the Province, public faith will be injured, the peace of the country broken, and it will be asked with eagerness "What could have induced His Majesty's Council to plunge a quiet and well ordered Province into

such a state?" and the answer will be received with
wonder and amazement. "To save the consumer of
brandy fourpence a gallon, and to gratify the importers
of that article." Will it not be a difficult matter of belief?
Will it not be said that this is not a matter of pence but
of principle? That those who wish well to the country
would not destroy its revenue for such a paltry question?
and will it not be said that it is high time the people of
this Province were turning their attention to the constitution of that body which has brought these evils upon
them? I maintain it Mr. Chairman, that Brandy is of all
others the fittest subject for taxation. That class of the
community who drink it are able to pay. It is not the
drink of the poor man, and to say that the duty cramps
the trade is ridiculous. It is the consumer and not the
merchant who pays the duty, and any other doctrine at
this day will not be believed.

*   *   *   *   *   *   *   *   *

When I find it necessary to review the proceedings
of the other branch of the Legislature, no motives of delicacy shall prevent me from expressing my sentiments.
I am always accustomed to do so in temperate and plain
language. I know and respect the members of that
Honorable Body individually, and some of them claim
my esteem, but it is their public conduct in their legislative capacity I am now considering. Mr. Chairman we
are guardians of the rights of the people of Nova Scotia.
A high and important trust is committed to us, and we
must watch with jealousy any step which may trench
further on the few privileges they retain. Sir, I have
ever felt it my duty, as a member of the House and particularly as its Speaker, to respect the rights of His
Majesty, and the privileges of the Council: I have been

friendly to the separate consideration of every subject by
each branch of the public service, and when each House
respects the views of the other, this mode may be prac-
ticed with advantage, but when I speak of separate
services, I do not mean such a detail as we have been
obliged to submit to during the present session. When
the small sums of money distributed throughout the
country for the roads and bridges have been watched
with a scrutinizing eye; when our subdivision has been
rejected because it did not suit the views of His Majesty's
Council; when the wants of the country which are best
known to us only are to be supplied with other hands;
when not only the appropriation of the public money is
attempted to be wrested from us, but when the Council
force upon us their suggestions; nay, when they dictate
to us the amount and mode of raising the revenue, is it
not time for us to pause and resume our rights? Sir,
when we submit to these encroachments, the rights and
privileges of the people we represent will become a
shadow and a name : when we return to our homes we
should act the part of honest men—we should tell them
not to be deceived ; that their representatives possess
neither power or influence, to address no more idle petitions to make known their wants, to inform us of the state
of the country, their roads or their bridges, but to alter
the address and send them to the other end of the build-
ing, if happily the Honorable Council may make provision
for them. Tell them that they are no longer to submit
to a revenue raised by their representatives, but to a scale
of duties imposed by those whose salaries are paid from
the public treasury. This House formerly possessed a
salutary control over those officers of the Government
who had seats in His Majesty's Council, because their

salaries depended upon the Revenue Bills, and anxious were they indeed to have those bills sent them from the Assembly. But now I will ask what control has this House over the Council? By permanent bills we have provided permanent salaries, and since the passing of the Imperial Act, a Revenue is raised without the aid of this House independent of the Province Laws, and independent of this House. Sufficient sums are collected and paid into the Treasury for the payment of the officers of Government, and here arises the indifference on the part of His Majesty's Council to the ordinary means of raising money for the public service; and hence the destruction of our constitutional control; it is now reduced to a name, and the proceedings of the other branch of the Legislature render this truth every day more and more apparent. When our privileges are few, and our influence reduced, and on the decline, it is high time for us to exert ourselves and to watch with care over what remains. If we are this year to submit to the direction of the Council, as to the amount of duty upon brandy, we must be prepared next year to be told that champaigne stood too high: the year following Port and Maderia and all other wines, which now pay a high duty will follow in the order of exemption until we have nothing left. It is not therefore the sum but the principle for which I am contending. If, Sir, we have not the power to grant a supply to His Majesty, and provide for the great public services of the country without this humiliating dictation—If the roads and the bridges, the education, the agriculture, the fisheries, and the commerce of the country are of so little importance in the eyes of His Majesty's Council that they are to be sold for fourpence upon brandy, and we are without redress, let us adjourn our session and return to our homes, and not insult the people we pretend to represent with the mere mockery and the empty form of Legislation.

Sir, I have ever been the constant advocate of every measure which in my opinion was calculated to promote harmony, so desirable in Legislation; but when peace is only to be purchased by the abandonment of right, I will not accept it on such terms. When the question of the Quit Rents was before the House I independently advocated the side which I judged right, and voted with the minority. That question has been disposed of, and I bow to the decision of the House; and although I differed with many members on that occasion, I nevertheless respect their opinion. I hope they may be right, and that I may be mistaken. It was a subject upon which we might well differ. It was one in which the rights of the Crown were involved, and this is one involving the privileges of the people, which I will not readily consent to abandon. Independently of my office in this House, which places me in the highest representative situation in the Province, all that I possess, my property and my friends, are here. These form the surest pledge that I will not willingly allow the country to be prejudiced by any act of mine. I would not willingly impose burdens on my children or my friends. This is my native land and my home, and here I expect to spend the remainder of my days, if it remains a free country, but if its freedom is lost, or if it is to be governed by a majority of five in His Majesty's Council, which I regard as the same thing, I would travel from it as from the city of Destruction.

*   *   *   *   *   *   *   *   *

Mr. Chairman, I came to this question without premeditation. I speak the sentiments which suggest themselves upon the occasion. I have heard the independent opinion of others, and when I am called upon in committee, upon the general state of the Province, I shall be prepared to deliver my opinion of men and measures more fully than is at present necessary. I have heard a rumour of dissolution spread within these walls. Whenever the Representative of His Majesty sees fit to dissolve this House, with him lies the responsibility, and let it be done, but let not the sound of it be heard within these walls to intimidate members. Upon those around me it can produce no effect, upon me the sound is lost. I know not the influence of terror: I will take no step here that I cannot justify to my constituents, whenever the day shall arrive that I am to meet them; but unless this House - possesses greater influence in the Legislature than it does at present, little honor will attach to a seat within its walls.

I may venture to say without fear of contradiction, that no man in this Assembly has exerted himself more than I have done to preserve the peace and order of the Colony: and no man has been more successful than myself in that particular, indeed so far have I gone, that I have not escaped censure for my unwearied efforts in this cause, but those who suppose that I will not make a stand when I consider the rights of this House invaded, know me not, and if I consider principle involved, I will not yield. The People of this country know my services and my disposition for peace. The Government on this and on the other side of the Atlantic know me, and they well know that I would not complain without just cause. No man would lament more than myself the interruption of harmony between the different branches of the Legislature, and I trust and hope a good understanding may be, even yet, preserved, but whilst the measures of the House in money matters, are opposed and rendered abortive by a majority of five members of His Majesty's Council, with little consideration for the feelings of the Representatives, tell not the inhabitants of Nova Scotia that they enjoy a free government. The voice of their Representatives is overborn and rendered of no avail when it militates in the slightest degree with the views of the Council. From the course pursued, the minority of this House have it in their power frequently to defeat the measures of the majority. I have been led to say more upon this subject than I intended. The Course pursued by His Majesty's Council was so unprecedented and so unexpected that it has called forth these observations. Again I request the House to judge for themselves, to pause and to deliberate, and what they determine, it shall be my endeavour as their Speaker to carry into effect."

We have made these copious extracts from this speech to show its general tenor and drift. Evidently it was delivered without premeditation. In a subsequent speech made on the same day, in reply to Mr. Uniacke, he says he felt it his duty to make some reply to what had fallen from the Honorable Gentleman from Cape Breton. "It has been said, Sir, that I have made a passsionate appeal to the feelings of this House, but this I take the liberty to deny. When I came here this morning it was with a determination to do my duty to the House, and to the Country.

I came not to make a speech, and what the Hon. Gentleman, who has so warmly espoused the side of H. M. Council, is pleased to call a passionate appeal, is nothing more than the free and temperate expression of my sentiments upon this important occasion. The Hon.

Gentleman has told us that the rights and privileges of
H. M. Council have been denied in this House. I. for
one, Mr. Chairman, am disposed to respect the privileges
of that Branch of the Legislature, but at the same time I will
watch with a jealous eye, that they do not encroach upon
the privileges of this House. No one has heard me yet
assert that the Council had not the right to reject the bill.
It is the expediency of exercising that right—the time
and the manner of rejecting the supply, against which I
complain. I ask was it politic, was it wise, did it evince
a due regard for the interests of the country, and the
rights of the people, to destroy by this Act the revenue
upon which our prosperity depends? The learned gentleman had talked much about our honor, but what has personal honor to do with the question? We are not sent
here to pay compliments. As a representative of the
people I allow no private interests, and no personal considerations, to dictate a course of conduct prejudicial to
their rights. I am not sent here to redress my own
grievances, or speak my private sentiments, but to
express the feelings of my constituents, to protect their
interests, and guard their rights.

* * * * * * * * *

The power of this House to grant a revenue is substance and not form. The means are ours, and we alone
are to determine how much we will voluntarily offer to
the Government and those aids should be accepted when
liberally offered. And is it because we have tendered too
much, that those who stand between us and the representative of His Majesty, have rejected the terms and left the
country in difficulty and distress?

It is the time, the manner and the circumstances of
exercising this power, of which I chiefly complain, and

if we are to be driven step by step to the wall, when there, at least, I am determined to make a stand. Consequences most serious to the people of this country will follow if we are to be used merely as a machine in the hands of His Majesty's Council, to prepare the Revenue Bills in the manner they shall dictate to us."

The effect produced by these speeches upon those who heard them, may be estimated by observations of the other gentlemen who took part in the debate, or listened to it.

Mr. Stewart said " he had thought of some mode of conciliating matters, but the speech he had listened to, had convinced him that there was but one course before the House."

Mr. Murdoch " was proud to recognize the talent and independence displayed on this occasion by the Honorable Speaker, he was proud to claim such a man as a native of the soil."

Mr. Young, who was not usually very partial to the Speaker was nevertheless obliged to say that he " had opened the controversy with admirable skill, and had arranged everything in such perfect and lucid order that he had left nothing untouched which could either illustrate or fortify his argument."

Mr. Uniacke, on whom the work fell of defending the Council. complimented Mr. Archibald on " the splendid eloquence with which he had enlightened the House."

Mr. Howe, the youthful editor of the Nova Scotian, who had lately begun his editorial career, but who had already shown the power of terse and vigorous expression which afterwards formed so striking a feature in his writings and speeches, in referring to the discussion which he had listened to and reported, says that " the

stand which Mr. Archibald had taken, and the two brilliant speeches which he had delivered in defence of the
House, had placed him on an elevation, which in the
whole course of his public life he had never before attained;
by his splendid and graceful oratory, his sound reasoning
and manly independence he had vindicated the title of
first commoner of his country."

While this discussioE was going on in the Lower
House the Council were not unconcerned spectators.
The reports of the speeches were carefully scanned, and on
the 7th April the Attorney General Mr. Uniacke, called the
attention of the Council to what purported to be reports
of speeches in the House. He alluded particularly to
the speech of *a* Mr. Dill, the substance of which we have
already given, but the great subject of offence was Mr.
Archibalds observation in which he charged the Council
with having invited the House to a mock Conference, the
bill on which it had been held having been already rejected. This he considered a charge of duplicity against
the Council. Doubtless it was, but Mr. Uniacke did not
venture to deny the fact. The Journals of his own House
proved it. The Council notwithstanding agreed unanimously to a series of thirteen Resolutions condemning
the speeches as containing "gross, scandalous, and libell-
ous charges against the Board and against the Members
thereof," and calling on the House to punish the offend-
ing members. This unfortunate message reached the
House while one of the three friends of the Council in
that Body was in the middle of a long harangue, proving
by extracts from writers on Constitutional Law, that the
Council were quite right in the exercise of the authority
they had asserted. An ordinary Speaker would have
been disconcerted by the interruption, but Mr. Barry had

ever since he had been expelled from the House in a previous session, been in the habit of delivering long and
prosy orations made up of extracts from books and papers.
Some of the speakers characterized him as the man who
carried his brains in his pocket. After the message Mr.
Barry went on with his speech. The other members
were thinking only of the message, and of what was to be
done with it. Mr. Barry was followed by some other
members who spoke with great force and animation. At
the close of the debate Mr. Archibald spoke again. We
append a few extracts from his Speech.

He said " I will address the House without any of
that warmth of temper which is so apparent upon the
other side, and notwithstanding the high crimes and mis-
demeanors with which I stand charged by His Majesty's
Council, I shall deliver my opinions as cooly and as
moderately as if the thundering dispatch which we lately
heard read, had never been delivered at our Bar. I am
not to be frightened into silence, or tamed into submis-
sion by such charges as I have listened to this day. I
look but to the rectitude of my intentions, to the good
sense and moderation, the brilliant tallants and manly independence which I find associated with me on this question. I need not particularize where all have been so distinguished and successful, but I may be permitted to say
that I am proud to find that great occasions are only want-
ing to call forth great talents and great exertions in Nova
Scotia.

I am proud to see that the minds which are usually
employed upon the common ordinary business of this
Assembly can when great constitutional questions call
them into action, exhibit powers which do honor to this
House and to the Country. I am not a speechmaker,

Mr. Chairman, it has never been my habit to commit to paper or to memory anything which I may find it necessary to offer this House. I trust to nothing but the general knowledge I possess and what may arise within my mind upon the spur of the moment, and as the occasion may seem to require. I do not, like my Honorable friend from Shelburne, resort to scraps of paper for my arguments, nor attempt to weigh down a debate with a motley array of extracts from all the books, into which chance, or the course of my studies, may have led me to look. When I see myself associated in this cause with such men as my Honorable friend from the Town of Halifax, the Honorable and learned gentleman from Cumberland, and the Honorable member from Sydney, and when I see on all sides around me, men who if not accustomed to mix in debate, or to clothe their sentiments in language, are nevertheless possessed of shrewd minds and good sound sense and judgement: and when I see that they have taken a stand and come to a decision on a full view of this question and of the general state of the Province, I think I require no other answer to my Honorable friends on the other side who accuse me of *leading the House astray.* I would be ashamed of this house if I thought for one instant that a speech, however brilliant, could turn the heads of members. I have not the magic influence which has been ascribed to me. I speak a plain language, and it is addressed to the reason. Sir, if it had been the general wish of this House to yield up its privileges, if it had been resolved to make a bargain with His Majesty's Council, and to patch up this unconstitutional infraction, I, as the servant of this House must have submitted to this decision. But that was not the feeling of this House. Before I opened my lips in the

Committee, a feeling of indignation pervaded the general mind and many members had given expression to that feeling.

It has been said that I have overstepped my duty in standing forward upon this occasion, but, Sir, suppose I remained silent in the Committee, or retired into my chamber, and left the House to settle the question as they could, should I have done my duty to this House or to the Country? Would it not have been remarked as singular and unmanly that the Speaker should desert his post in the hour of difficulty and danger, and when the question was asked "Where is the Speaker?" it would be answered, "he has retired to his chamber." How could members stand forward with confidence, in this great constitutional struggle, if they found it avoided by the Speaker, the natural guardian of the rights and privileges of this House? Sir, I will make my voice to be heard, till it is acknowledged that we possess a right, which to an Englishman and a freeman, is the dearest of all rights, *that of taxing ourselves, without the intervention or dictation of any power upon earth.*

When in the chair yesterday, I listened with great attention to my Honorable friend from the County of Cape Breton, and I thank him for the manner in which my conduct and arguments were treated. I can easily appreciate the feelings which led him to defend his venerable father, and let it not be supposed for a moment, that, while contending against a public Body for principles in which the public are concerned, I would make any charge derogatory to the character of its members; or single out any gentleman for the purpose of gratuitous or uncalled for attack. I have never known a father. Unfortunately for me, mine died in a foreign land when I was an in-

fant, but I honor the impulse which leads a son to defend
his parent even from suspicion. In my remarks on a
former day, I could not have alluded to the Honorable
Gentleman's father, for this plain reason, that his salary,
like my own, does depend upon the appropriation Bill—
and he will not be paid, nor I either, in consequence of
the failure of the Revenue Bill. The general strain of my
argument was, that all the officers of the Government
ought to be dependant for their salaries upon the Revenue
granted by the people—and when they are so, the natural consequence is, that they must all feel an interest in
securing a Revenue Bill. Will any one tell me that if
the salaries depended entirely upon this Bill, this, nevertheless, would have no effect? If there is anyone mad
enough to make such an assertion, where, I would ask, is
the man to be found, who would be fool enough to believe it?—

*   *   *   *   *   *   *   *   *

My disposition has ever been for peace, my habits
as a public man have been of the most forbearing and
quiescent character. I have never failed to advocate, by
the aid of reason and argument the rights both of the
King and of the people, whenever I found they were
attacked. I have acted upon this principle, *that the interests and happiness of the people are best subserved, by pre-
serving the just rights and prerogatives of the Crown, and that
I best discharge my duty to my King, when I uphold the rights
and promote the happiness of his people.*

It has been my misfortune to have my views and intentions more misrepresented than any other man in the
country, but I have the consolation to know that my
course has been plain, conscientious, and upright. I may
have erred, as other men err,—but I am willing to place

my public conduct in comparison with that of any other public servant, and to be judged by the world.

* * * * * * * * *

I will now turn to the Journals of the House at the period when the venerable Chief Justice was the Speaker. As, on a former day, I drove His Majesty's Council from the records of the Lords and Commons, I will now show that the Journals of this House will not afford the slightest ground for their pretensions. I will show that, at that early day, the spirit of British freedom and constitutional liberty was engrafted upon this Assembly. That spirit will grow with our growth, and strengthen with our strength, but never, with my consent, shall it grow into licentiousness. If I saw any such tendency, I would oppose it. I would say at once to this house "Stand here, I will advance no further." Liberty and right are what I wish and nothing more. It really appears to me that there is something singular in the atmosphere of the Council Chamber, that men of the most liberal sentiments become immediately changed the moment they take their seats there. (Here the Hon. Gentleman read from the Journals the address of the House to the Governor in 1790,) of which the following in an extract. "It is one of the inherent privileges of the House that all money bills should originate with them, and that no interference of the Council by attempting to make alterations in them should be admitted : this inherent privilege the House of Assembly are determined to maintain, as essential to their very existence. They are nevertheless extremely concerned that their struggle for an undoubted privilege should be the means of throwing the public into confusion, and of depriving His Majesty of an annual and efficient Revenue of near Ten Thousand Pounds." This is a case precisely in point. They go with us step by step, but there is the difference that instead of £10,000, we sustain a loss of £30,000, (reads again) "We trust your Excellency will do us the justice to believe that every measure consistent with our duty has been taken on our parts to prevent so great a calamity: and we have no doubt when your Excellency shall have perused the minutes of our proceedings, which we now beg leave to lay before your Excellency for that purpose, the *House of Assembly* will stand fully acquitted of every degree of culpability in this respect."

I will now turn your attention to another case, when the Attorney General was Speaker of the House (here he read from the Resolutions of the House in 1799) "The House of Assembly appeal, to the feelings of His Majesty's Council, very many of whom have heretofore been members of the same House, and pray H. M. Council, but for a moment to consider with what astonishment they received from H. M. Council a declaration that it was the right of H. M. Council to frame money bills equally with the House of Assembly. Could the House of Assembly be base enough to surrender the privileges transmitted to them by their ancestors, the exercise of such a right, could only embarrass H. M. Council, and bring H. M. Government into disregard and disrepute among his subjects.

The House of Assembly unanimously avow that it is the sole inherent and unalienable right of the Representatives of the People to frame and originate all money bills; and that it is the law and constitution of Great Britain, so established from time immemorial, and that such right is one of the main pillars of the British constitution, and is a right which British subjects will never surrender, but with their lives. Were the House of Assembly to attempt to offer reasons or precedents to show, that this claim is well founded, it might imply the possibility of there being a doubt upon the subject. His Majesty's Council claiming the right, or giving it up, cannot change that which is already fixed and established.

The wisdom and good understanding of H. M. Council will convince them that the declaration of a right will by no means establish or create such right, and that it can answer no good purpose but to create uneasiness in the minds of His Majesty's subjects, and to disturb the harmony of the several branches of the Ligislature,—which is so essentially necessary for the support and honor of His Majesty's Government."

Has this language, I would ask, no meaning ? Are these mere empty words ? The wisdom and good understanding of H. M. Council will teach them that it is the language of men jealous of their rights, and determined to uphold them. This then is not the first time the people of Nova Scotia have been obliged to step forth and assert their rights. I read these passages, especially for the edification of my Hon. and learned friend from Cape Breton, and let me ask, with such examples before me, could I pursue a different course, and allow my name to go down to posterity in the continuation of the same Journals with ignominy and disgrace ? I have been accused, Mr. Chairiman, of using language offensive to H. M. Council. Few men can teach me lessons in moderation or propriety, and I am anxious not to infringe parliamentary rules. I will keep myself free to remark in such terms as I consider appropriate, upon the acts and conduct of the other branch of the Legislature ; and I hold myself accountable to no man for the due exercise of my privileges as a member of this House. Freedom of action is the birthright of every freeman, and freedom of speech is the undoubted right of the representatives of the people. I am accustomed to express myself in a temperate and plain manner, and I deny that I have used any unparliamentary or improper language. I have not seen the paper complained of, but if my remarks are correctly reported I am ready to avow and I will never retract them. Do H. M. Council think that the extraordinary course they have pursued is to pass unnoticed and without comment? It is my privilege to canvass their measures and, upon an occasion like this, I am not disposed to waive it. My views and conduct have already been misrepresented, and I doubt not will be so again. To such charges I reply with the ancient Philosopher, " I live every day to contradict them." I am ready and able to defend myself; and Sir, there is but one quarter from which trouble may come when I will be silent. What do I find Mr. Chairman that this last unprecedented message of H. M. Chuncil was *unanimously* resolved? Where was my Hon. friend the Master of Rolls * on this occasion? Was he present, and is he so changed by the atmosphere of the Council Chamber, that he has entirely forgotten the language he was wont to use, and the conduct he pursued in this House? Did I not hear him, Mr. Chairman, from that seat cooly and deliberately, not warmed as I have been in debate, and goaded by an intemperate opposition, proclaim, that H. M. Council were an ephemeral body, created by the breath of the King and destroyed at his pleasure, and is he now the first to take offence at language of a vastly different nature? Has he forgotten the time when he presided in this House? and has he joined

* Mr. Robie, former Speaker.

the cry against the Speaker for standing forth to defend the rights of the people ? Proud am I to say, Mr. Chairman, that the venerable Chief Justice, the President of that board, was not present at these unanimous deliberations."

On the 8th April, the Committee of the whole reported an address to the President, setting forth the case from their point of view. This passed in a House of thirty five by a majority of twenty nine, there being thirty two for and three against it.

The minority were Mr. Uniacke, Mr. Hartshorne and Mr. Barry.

Two days after the close of the debate on the address, a Committee of the House reported an answer to the memorandum of the Council in reference to the complaints of that Body as to the speeches made in the Assembly, asserting, that though they were ready to uphold the dignity of the Council, the opinions expressed by that Body, and the uncourteous terms in which they were expressed precluded the House from noticing them.

This answer was ordered to be sent to the Council by the usual majority.

In their answer to the memorandum from the Council they took no notice of the charge against Mr. Archibald, but on the same day they passed another resolution with only three dissentients, stating that the House entertained the highest esteem for the talents integrity and ability of the Honorable Speaker, whose public conduct had secured him the confidence of the house and the Country.

Nothing was said about "a Mr. Dill" the other offender. No answer could be given to the sneer conveyed by the indefinite article, and the House did not attempt it.

On the 13th April the Administrator came down to the House and prorogued it.

He said that though eight weeks had elapsed since they met, the most important measures remained in abeyance " in consequence of differences of opinion on points which had long been established, and recognized as necessary for the satisfactory and effectual conducting of the affairs of a Government constituted as ours is."

What this means it would be hard to say. What were the points that were established ? and were they established as the House or as the Council understood them? Mr. Wallace was evidently driven to take shelter under a vagueness of phraseology which each House might read in ts own way. Had not both branches united in a practical assertion of the hereditary right of the family, to the office of Treasurer ?

But whatever doubt his speech might have left on the audience, it would have been removed, if they could have had a sight of the Despatch which he sent to Sir George Murray, eight days afterwards, in which he told the Colonial Secretary, that he saw nothing could be done but to prorogue the House till the first July, when Sir Peregrine would be back, and would see the necessity of a dissolution, since ' from what had passed during the late Session, it appeared to him no business could be done satisfactorily with it."

Sir Peregrine did return about the middle of June, but seems not to have decided upon that course, for he prorogued the House by a Proclamation issued immediately after his return and dated the twenty first of June. Five days afterwards occurred an event which saved him from embarrassment. He was not indeed aware of the fact till the fourth of August following, but George IV

had died on the 26th June, and the Assembly was *ipso
facto* dissolved. Writs for a new Election were issued returnable the 8th November. The excitement at this
election exceeded anything that ever before had been
known in this Province.

CHAPTER VI.

President reports to Colonial Minister. Speaker does same.
President writes to Under Secretary of Colonies. Reply. Mr.
Archibald declines Judgeship. Council's friends disappointed
with Mr. Archibald's course. Reasons assigned. Curious letter in the Free Press. Conjectures as to its authorship. Dis-
section of letter. Consideration of reasons assigned by letter
writer.

At the close of the first session of 1830, when the
House rose, it was the duty of Mr. Wallace to report the
proceedings to his superiors in England. The Speaker
felt assured they would be represented in no favorable
light to himself and the majority of the House. He ventured therefore to give his own version of them in a
communication addressed directly to the Colonial Office.
This did not pass, as such documents should, by the rules
of the Department, through the Lieutenant Governor. In
it he discloses and defends the grounds on which the
majority had taken their stand in the controversy.

Mr. Wallace seems to have heard of this letter, and
complains of it as an irregular proceeding, in a dispatch
dated the 15th June, 1830, addressed by him to Mr. Hay,
the Under Secretary at the Colonial Office. That gentleman in his reply evades the complaint, but expresses
the hope of Lord Bathurst that some plan will be hit
upon to reconcile the differences between the two
branches of the Legislature.

Mr. Archibald was then Solicitor General. He was
subject to dismissal at the pleasure of the Crown. To be
sure, the salary attached to the office was but trifling,
and, moreover, such as it was, it depended on an annual
vote of the Legislature. There could, therefore, be no
great object in depriving him of a position which at best

had but small emolument, and that subject to the contingency of an annual vote. Clearly, then, it was not any regard for his Crown office, that induced him to go out of the usual course in such cases, and open a correspondence with the Colonial Office, but, as Government was then constituted, the Council being a unit against him, he felt that his future largely depended on his standing in the Department, and that he needed to defend himself against the secret representations of a Governor under the control of the Council, and of an Administrator who was himself a member of Council, and breathed its spirit. This paper doubtless had its effect, in connexion with similar communications from New Brunswick, in paving the way for a dispatch from Lord Bathurst on the subject of a re-construction of the Council, of which we shall have occasion by and by to speak more at length.

On the 5th of February Mr. Stewart, one of the Puisne Judges, died. The office was kept open during the session. At the close, it was offered to Mr. Archibald, who declined it. He could not honorably, even if disposed, desert his friends by accepting office at a time when a controversy, largely due to his exertions, was at its height, but, independently of this consideration, the Puisne Judgeship was not the object of his ambition, and the less so that it was henceforth, by a policy recently adopted at the Colonial Office, to be dissociated from a seat in the Council.

On his declining the office, it was offered to and accepted by Mr. R. J. Uniacke, who had deserved well of the Government by his able advocacy of their interests in the House.

Shortly after came the election of 1830.

The course which Mr. Archibald had for some years
pursued in the Legislature, as regards the Council, had
been so courteous and considerate, that his action on the
brandy question was the occasion of great disappointment
and annoyance to that Body. The friends of the Council
soon set to work to find out reasons for this change of
attitude. They asserted that his course was quite inconsistent with the doctrines he had advocated in Prince
Edward Island while President of the Council of that
Colony. He had, therefore, it was said, not only changed
his attitude towards the Upper House, but had abjured
his own declared opinions. What could be the cause of
such a result? The *Free Press*, the organ of the Council,
had no hesitation in giving it. Mr. Archibald was offended with the Judge and the Attorney General for the
efforts they were making to secure for one of themselves
the office at which he also was aiming. It was his indignation and resentment, when he perused the contents
of the misdirected letter that induced him to break with
the Council, and lead on a party against them. The
whole story is told with the most minute details, in a
communication to the Free Press, from which we have
already quoted some passages. This letter deserves dis-
section for various reasons, and we shall proceed to examine it with some particularity. The article is not particularly coherent. The writer shifts his ground in the
course of his remarks, not only in his ascription of motives, but also on another point to which we shall allude
further on. He begins his letter by stating the motive
which governed Mr. Archibald in the course he took.
This he alleges to be " self-interest which never slumbers
nor sleeps",—he does not pretend to show in what way
Mr. Archibald's interest was to be promoted by engaging

in the controversy.   Indeed he has hardly made the assertion before he abandons it—and then proceeds to assign
another and totally different reason.   He relates the particulars of the interview between the judge and Attorney
General on the one side, and Mr. Archibald on the other, the
details of which we have already noticed, and then goes
on to state that Mr. Archibald left the conference in
temper, and was then " no doubt deeply impressed that
His Majesty's Council made a direct inroad on the rights
and privileges of the House of Assembly, by questioning
the right of the speaker to the Chief Justiceship of the
Province"—That on the perusal of the ominous letter he
made the wonderful discovery that in His Majesty's
Council, " the chains were forged and the fetters prepared
to be thrown round our necks and those of our children"
and test mere expressions unaccompanied by proof might
seem, to the discerning, but empty sounds—the chimera
of a disordered imagination, goaded by disappointed ambition, the whole Province must be deprived of their revenue and appropriation, as proof positive that these
rights and liberties were sacrificed."   That they had
been sacrificed who would deny?   Not, however, by
His Majesty's Council but by those who had sworn to
protect them, and for what reason?   Because, forsooth, the Attorney General of the Province would
presume to compete for an office to which, according to
the customs and usages of Great Britain, he had a better
right and claim than Mr. Archibald could possibly have by
any other consideration."   This letter purports to be written on the " best authority."   It states the facts of the interview with Mr. Archibald, the communication to Sir
John Coape Sherbrooke, and the fate of his answer with a
minuteness savoring of personal knowledge, or informa-

tion derived from persons having that knowledge ; and the letter, on the face of it, bears the marks of being written in the interest of Mr. Uniacke. According to it, *he* is the person who, by the usage and custom of Great Britain, would be entitled to the falling office. Indeed the statement is made in language almost identical with that which Sir Peregrine had used in his Bermuda letter, enclosing the Attorney General's papers to the Colonial Office. It is language which Sir Peregrine had probably borrowed from the letter of Mr. Uniacke, forwarding these papers to Bermuda. All this would lead to the inference that Mr. Uniacke might fairly have been sus- pected of being himself the writer of the letter, if there were no internal evidence in the document, to lead to a different conclusion. Now, is there any such evidence ? First, let us enquire as to the nationality of the writer. He speaks of Mr. Archibald, making the wonderful dis- covery, that in His Majesty's Council "the fetters were forged to be thrown round our necks and those of our children." Surely there is something peculiarly Irish in the idea of "*fetters*" being intended for "*necks.*" An Englishman might have thought of a yoke for the neck, but surely would have applied *fetters* to the *feet.* Then there is in the rich exuberance of the phrase, " the chimera of a disordered imagination," something which smacks of a Celtic origin. And when the writer goes further with his imagery, who but an Irishman could conceive the idea of *disappointed ambition* applying a *goad* to a *chimera ?* We think, therefore, there is strong in- ternal evidence to shew that the writer was an Irishman. It remains to be ascertained what Irishman it was.

As we have already said, the startling resemblance between the language of the article in the newspaper, and that of Sir Peregrine's letter, not then published, goes a long way to shew that the words in both cases were derived from the same source. But there is something to strengthen this inference. The article, commences as an argument for the Judge, as well as the Attorney General. It goes to shew that either of them had a better right than Mr. Archibald, but as the writer proceeds and warms up, he quietly drops the Judge, and in accounting for Mr. Archibald's temper, says that it arose from the idea " *that, forsooth, the Attorney General would presume to compete for the Chief Justiceship.*" What has become of the Judge? The writer no longer recollects that there is such a person in the controversy. Could any one but an Irishman make such a blunder? And could any Irishman make it except one so blinded, to use the writer's phrase, by " self interest which never slumbers nor sleeps," as not to recollect how he had commenced his argument? In the beginning of the communication there were two antagonists to Mr. Archibald's pretensions. Now there is but one. Mr. Uniacke, in his mind's eye, sees only himself.

But then it might be said that the Attorney General could not write a letter so little coherent as this is. Mr Uniacke certainly was a man of very considerable ability —he had great force of character—he was an eloquent speaker, but he never was remarkable for the logical accuracy of his reasoning. Mr. Archibald used to tell a laughable story which illustrates this feature of Mr. Uniacke's mind. He had published an edition of the permanent Statutes from 1759 to 1804, and had prepared a copious index to the volume. On one occasion in Court it became necessary to turn up the Statute on the subject of *Administrators.* The index was referred to, but in vain.

The word *administrators* was not to be found. Mr.
Uniacke himself was in Court and was applied to. He
was asked under what head the law was to be found. He
replied under the head of *Wills*. "Precisely," said
Mr. Archibald, look under *wills* because there is *no*
will. If you want *rain* look for it under *sunshine*
Such was the style of Mr. Uniacke's mind. The inco-
herency in the letter, the want of logical sequence, the
shifting of the motive power, from self interest to passion,
the setting out with three aspirants for office and ending
with two, instead of being evidence against, are really
evidence in favor of the conjecture, as to the authorship
of this letter. We do not by any means venture to assert
that Mr. Uniacke wrote it, but what we do say is, that
many a poor fellow has been hanged on circumstantial
evidence much less conclusive.

Now, let us examine both these theories of self
interest and temper,—and see what there is to support
either. Let us take the temper first. This is said to
have arisen on the perusal of the "*ominous letter*" from
Sir J. C. Sherbrooke. Now why should Mr. Archibald be
angry? He knew as well before, as he did after, the receipt of that letter, that the Judge and the Attorney
General were both seeking the office. It was a matter of
certainty that each would use every means in his power
to secure the coveted prize. The letter could not add to
his knowledge of these facts. It is quite true that it gave
him more specific details of what was being done than he
would otherwise have had, but what then? So far from
being angry about the matter, he must have been exceed-
ingly amused to find that the particular friend of his
antagonists had forwarded a full statement of all they
were doing to the very man from whom they would have

been most anxious to withhold the information. The letter did not mention that an appointment had been decided on. Had that been the case, Mr. Archibald might have felt very much disappointed. But that result was not reached for two years to come. But even supposing Mr. Archibald to have been deeply offended and unreasonable enough to quarrel with Mr. Halliburton and Mr. Uniacke, it would be absurd in him to visit the offence, not on the men who he thought had wronged him, but on the innocent people of Nova Scotia. What need had Mr. Halliburton to care for the loss of the tariff? His salary was secure. It was charged in the revenue of the Crown, and would be paid if not a shilling was levied under the Act. And as for the Attorney General, if his salary was partly, Mr. Archibald's own was wholly, derived from the vote of the Legislature. He could not injure the Judge, nor could he injure the Attorney General without suffering himself. The assumption, therefore, that Mr. Archibald was acting from temper, and aiming to avenge himself on the other men who were competing with him for office, is too absurd to bear the slightest scrutiny.

Then as to the other assumed motive—that of self interest—there is still less reason for that view. His interest was entirely opposed to the course he pursued. If he had thought of that, his policy would have been very different. The Colonial Minister would not care to reward a man who had thrown himself into active opposition to the King's Representative in the Colony, who had assailed a body of men on whom the Minister mainly relied for advice in the exercise of his patronage in the Province,—who had thrown the local finances into confusion, who had cast upon the Crown the necessity of providing for local officials, out of the territorial revenues, already straitened by the charges borne on them. It would be a very odd way of promoting his interest with the Minister to thwart and embarrass him. But even then, how could Mr. Archibald suppose that those results would happen by the Assembly carrying out in the Bill the views they entertained? That body might be unwise in their views. Brandy might have been left to bear only the shilling, which the Council were willing to impose upon it, but could the Assembly, could Mr. Archibald have expected that the Council would be mad enough to take the course they did? True, they had declared that the extra fourpence was a burden too great for commerce to bear, They had proclaimed it as their aim to make that article fourpence a gallon cheaper than "it would be under the Bill," still, could the House, could anybody, believe that twelve elderly men, experienced in public affairs, comprising some of the best intellects in the country, would for such a reason throw away £40,000 of the public revenue? They certainly did make up their minds to do so. But then is there not as much ground to impute their course to temper, as to charge it upon Mr. Archibald or on any member of the Lower House? Whether it was temper or not, the House, at all events, were within their privileges, the Council without theirs.

CHAPTER VII.

Election of 1830. Candidates. Mr. Archibald's speech at Truro.
Meeting of House. Death of Attorney General Uniacke. Of-
fice kept open. Passage of Revenue Bill. Lord Goderich's
Despatch. Mission of Judge Halliburton to England. Mr.
Archibald appointed acting Attorney General. Visits England.
Judge Halliburton's and Mr. Archibald's race in England.
Attentions in England. Marquis of Lansdown's offer. Rejected.
Lord Goderich proposes changes in Judiciary. House refuse.
Lord Goderich to Administrator. Conclusion of question of
Chief Justiceship. Correspondence thereon. Remarks on
mode of day for obtaining promotion. Reaction after 1830.
State of public opinion in 1835 and '36. Joe Warner's Letters.
General Election of 1837. Mr, Logan's candidacy. Mr.
Archibald's speeches at Truro. Returned to Assembly.

The results of the election might well be open to
doubt. The majority in the Assembly was overwhelming,
but it might not truly represent the popular feeling. The
stand against the Council, whether right or wrong, was
founded on an abstract doctrine. The result of that
stand, the loss of the revenue, was a concrete fact, and
came home to the people. They might be uncertain as
to the political theory, they could have no doubt as to
what they suffered in consequence. Roads and bridges
would fall into decay, and there was no money to repair
them. Packets and ferries, which could ply only when
aided by bounties from the Legislature, must either stop
or be continued at a sacrifice. The people would be sure
to feel the loss. Would they appreciate the spirit that
occasioned it? There were many who thought that a
sense of present evil would outweigh attachment to constitutional doctrine. So the parties went to the country,
the newspapers ranging themselves on one side or the
other, and making their prophesies as newspapers
generally do, in accord with what they wished to come

about. For the County of Halifax the nomination day
was the 12th September. The candidates for that county
were four on each side. Messieurs Archibald, Lawson,
Smith and Blanchard represented the views which had
prevailed in the last Assembly. Messieurs Hartshorne,
Barry, Starr and Blackadar those of the Opposition. The
various candidates addressed the electors at the hustings.
When the poll was removed to Truro, after it had been
kept open a week at Halifax, the electors were again addressed by the several candidates. Mr. Barry was the
last to speak on behalf of the views of the Council. That
gentleman, ever since his expulsion from the House, had
a grudge against Mr. Archibald who issued the warrant
in his case. He now took occasion to censure rather
severely the conduct of Mr. Archibald on the question at
issue between the Council and the House. At the close
of his speech, Mr. Archibald was the only candidate who
had not yet spoken. We subjoin one or two extracts from
his address on that occasion.

"I would not," said he, "occupy a moment of your
time, but something has dropped from the gentleman
who last addressed you to which I feel it my duty to reply. I will not attempt to flatter you, but this I may
with safety say, that the people of this district are an or-
derly and intelligent people. They read and think for
themselves. They form their own opinions upon such information as they can acquire, and are not to be influenced in their public conduct by any merely personal
considerations. It is upon principle that myself and my
friends now come to ask your support. I respect the
other candidates who sit beside me, and for some of them
I have a high regard, but they profess very different
principles from mine; principles which, I am satisfied,

will not meet with your approbation. If my own father, or my brother, were to come here. holding the principles which those gentlemen hold, I should vote against them. I will sanction no backstair communications with H. M. Council. I will represent freemen and the sons of freemen, or I will be no representative at all. We have heard from one gentleman a history of the constitution, but I will show you in a very few words that some material features have been omitted. As you all know, the knowledge which I have gained has been drilled into me in a school of adversity. I have had to study the constitution closely, that I might apply my knowledge to the business of the Province. I was nursed upon the brink of the stream which flows beside us, and I have had to fight my way through many obstacles, and have raised myself entirely by my own exertions to the distinguished office which I hold. And is it I who have been honored by His Majesty with the office of Solicitor General; am I the man who would strike at the Government of the country? who would unnecessarily disturb the Province, who would introduce anarchy to gratify any personal feelings? Mr. Barry has told you that too much has been said about the rights of the people. Sorry am I that, with some, they have become a bye word and a disgrace. But it is for no vague and undefined right that we have contended. Were I to see any disposition, either in the Legislature or out of it, to press matters to extremity, to go beyond the bounds of the constitution, I would be the first to say, Stop. Let us go no further. If you do I will not go with you. We have been told that our constitution is like that of England. It is for the rights and privileges of Englishmen that I contend and nothing more. You are the sons of Britons, of fathers

who came to this country, when it was a land of pits,
even as bad as the valley of the shadow of death. They
were, as I have often said, like a handful of corn scattered
upon the tops of the mountains. In those early periods
we had a little Council, which sat around a table and conducted the affairs of the Province, until His Majesty gave
us a constitution which secured to the people of this
Colony the full enjoyment of British liberty.

* * * * * * * * *

" I do not seek to degrade H. M. Council. I give them
a high pedestal. I place them on the same level as the
House of Lords, the hereditary Baronage of England.
But whenever the Council can so use their power as to
deprive us of the right of taxation, they may force us to
impose a land tax' or any other tax, which may be most
agreeable to their wishes. In the full consciousness of
the evils that might be brought upon us, I spake out my
sentiments without fear and without disguise. And what
are the consequences? Look to the poll book and see
how my name stands there. Scarcely a man in office, or
an expectant of office, had the hardihood to vote for me.

* * * * * * * * *

" I do not seek for your support on personal but
upon public grounds. If I had sold your rights, and sacrificed your authority, I might then come to you with a
tone of supplication and plead the kindnesses and the in-
timacies of private life, but I take a higher stand, and
ask you again to arm me in your defence, again to give
me the power of upholding your interests and the interests of my native country. I trust that you will give to
myself and my friends such a support as will enable us
again to take our seats in the Assembly, and show to the
world that the principles, which we laboured to maintain
have met your approbation."

Well did the people of Colchester justify the expectations expressed in this speech. On Saturday, when he left Halifax, Mr. Archibald was 300 below the highest opposition candidate. At the close of the Poll at Truro, he was 800 above him. Tne Poll was then adjourned to Pictou and at its close there, Mr. Archibald and his colleagues were returned by triumphant majorities.

The new House met on the 8th November. Mr. Uniacke, the Attorney General, had died a month before that date, but no announcement of the death appears to have been made to the Colonial Secretary till three weeks after the opening of the Session.

On the 29th November the Revenue Bill which had met so disasterous a fate in the previous Assembly was again brought forward. The old duty of 1s 4d. on Brandy was again proposed. When Sir Peregrine wrote his letter announcing the vacancy in the Attorney Generals Office, the bill had not yet come up for its second reading. It was uncertain by what majority it would pass in the House, or what might be its fate when it reached the Upper House. In the meanwhile care was taken that the great opponent of the Council should not profit by the vacancy, Sir Peregrine Maitland accordingly, in his letter to the Colonial Secretary, requested him to make no appointment to the office, and to give no promise of it, to anyone in the meantime. He added that at the close of the session he would address the Secretary more particularly on the subject. The office accordingly remained open till after the House rose.

The Bill soon passed through its several stages below without a division, and was sent to the Council on the 9th December. That body had watched the proceedings of the Lower House with care. They soon saw that it was impossible to fight the battle further, and prepared to yield. Within forty-eight hours after the Bill reached the Council it was sent back to the Assembly duly agreed to. The "Burden on Commerce," which had furnished the pretext for its rejection at last session, remained, but the point was no longer urged. The Council felt that they could not again enter on a fight for the four pence. It was bétter that commerce should bear the extra burden. They shrunk from further disturbing the finances by usurping a power which belonged to the Assembly. Indeed, the time was fast coming when, even to retain their unquestioned privileges, would require all the exertions they could use. That was not the time to encroach upon the privileges of the other House. While they were hesitating what course they should take when this Bill came before them, the Colonial Minister was contemplating an entire change in the constitution of the Provincial Councils. On the 7th December, 1830, he addressed Sir Peregrine on the subject. He said his attention had been directed to the composition of the Upper Branch in New Brunswick and Nova Scotia, and he proposed to give them a more independent character by introducing a larger number of members not holding office at the pleasure of the Crown. He wished the Governor to inform him whether the materials for a body of that description were to be found in Nova Scotia, and if so, to report the names of suitable persons. This dispatch must have arrived about the time of the close of the session, and seems to have excited great alarm among the members of H. M. Council. Accordingly, shortly after the close of the House, Judge Halliburton proceeded to England to defend the constitution of the body of which he was a prominent member. He is not, indeed, ostensibly commissioned

for that service.   On the contrary, he is accredited to the
Minister by Sir Peregrine, as the bearer of a joint address
of the two Houses to the Crown, remonstrating against
the reduction of the duties on foreign timber imported
into Great Britain.   Sir Peregrine explains why he had
sent the address by the Judge, instead of as usual by
mail, by saying that the Judge would be able to furnish
every information on the subject of the timber duties
which the Government might require.   It seems a little
odd that, on a question of trade, a delegate should not
have been selected from the Lower House.   It is still
more odd that on a matter of that kind, even if the selection were made from the Upper House, a merchant, or
man of business in that body, should not have been chosen.
The matter required a special knowledge of trade, yet the
choice fell on a gentleman who had never been in business, whose life had been spent in pursuits as alien as
possible from the trade in timber.   It is only when we
come to look at a subsequent letter of Sir Peregine Maitland, asking to have Judge Halliburton reimbursed for
the expenses of his trip to England, that we find out the
truth.   His business was only ostensibly the trade in
timber.   As a member of Council, he was really sent to
look after the interests of that Body, threatened in the
dispatch just referred to.   There is another letter of Sir
Peregrine to the same address, and bearing date the same
day, with the one introducing Judge Halliburton and his
timber business, which raises the inference, that besides
the defence of the Council's interests, he had an interest
of his own to look after, one which probably had more
to do with his being the delegate, than either the timber
duties or the constitution of the Council.   We have already mentioned the death of Attorney General Uniacke.

It took place on the 10th October. His office had re-mained vacant until the close of the session, but the courts were now coming on, and it was necessary to have some person to do the Crown business. Mr. Archibald was therefore made *acting* Attorney General, and the fact was only reported to England. This produced an alteration in the state of the question of the Chief-Justice-ship. Sir Peregrine, in his letter accompanying Mr. Uniacke's application, had stated his belief that in the sentiment and usage of the country, the holder of the Attorney General's office was entitled to succeed to the Chief-Justiceship, if it became vacant during his incum-bency. The new Attorney General was young, active, vigorous and able, a sound lawyer, and with a reputation for eloquence far exceeding that of any other Provincial lawyer. He was not only at the head of the Bar, but at the head of the Assembly, and possessed immense influ-ence in the country. Clearly it was necessary for the Judge to be on the alert, if he did not wish his claims to be overborne by the powerful influence wielded by his competitor. But the Judge had also strong claims. In character and attainments he was unimpeachable. A more honest and upright Judge never presided over a court, and he had the 'lucubrationes viginti annorum' necessary to constitute a great lawyer. Still, with such a competitor, he could not afford to neglect his suit. Accordingly we find him, a few days after the session closed, on his way across the Atlantic, to press his claims at Downing Street. But he was not allowed to remain there long alone. He is followed shortly afterwards by Mr. Archibald, who presents himself at the Colonial Of-fice. Whether the two gentlemen met each other in the anti-chamber of the office in Downing Street, or, if they did,

whether they conversed with each other on the subject of
timber duties, or the constitution of Colonial Councils, we
have no means of knowing, but we may rest assured
that there was one subject of which they did not speak, and
that was what was to happen when Mr. Blowers ceased
to be Chief-Justice.   The contest on the other side of the
Atlantic appears to have excited some amusement here.
A Halifax newspaper of the third of February contains a
dialogue between two imaginary persons on the subject
of the trip to England.   One of them says—"I hear a
Puisne Judge and an Attorney General of our Province
are to run a race from Liverpool to London for heavy
stakes—The flag of the former has the following motto.
"When the place of Chief Justice becomes vacant a
Puisne Judge, who has approved himself deserving should
be preferred."—*Bacon.*

The flag of the latter has this inscription,

"My friend will move the King, to any shape of preferment such as I'll desire."—*Shakspeare.*

In the previous year General Fox and his wife, who
was Lady Mary Fitzclarence, a daughter of King William, had been residing in Halifax and were on very
intimate terms with Mr. Archibald's family.   This is
probably what is alluded to as the Court influence on
which Mr. Archibald was supposed to lean.   At all events
when he went to England, he was accompanied by his
daughter then a young woman of great beauty and accomplishments, to whom he was most tenderly attached.
They received the greatest attention from their friends,
the General and Lady Mary, and were very much fêted
while they remained in London.   It seems that at this
time the Marquis of Lansdown, heard Mr. Archibald
speak at a public dinner, a task of which he always ac-

quitted himself well. The Marquis was so delighted with the wit and humor of the speech and its polished style, that he sought an acquaintance with him which soon ripened into friendship. Sometime afterwards the Marquis urged him to enter Parliament, and offered him one of the seats of Calne, a Borough which was in his gift, and urged Mr. Archibald to accept the offer, if it were only temporarily. The answer was characteristic. "No my Lord, said Mr. Archibald, I am already the head of one House, I do not care to become the tail of another."

The Colonial Minister appears to have had much difficulty in making up his mind on the subject of the Chief Justiceship. Both candidates left England with great uncertainty as to the result. In the end the influence of the representative of the Crown here, sustained by the Members of Council, all of whom were colleagues and friends and several of them relatives of Judge Halliburton, prevailed with the Minister. He did not however come to a conclusion for a long period. Over a year had passed, since the candidates had returned to Nova Scotia. At last on the 4th December 1832, Lord Goderich who now held the seals of Office, writes two dispatches addressed to the Administrator of the Government of Nova Scotia. That office was held at the time by Mr. Jeffrey. In one of these, he proposes a scheme for remodelling the Judiciary. Instead of five Judges then constituting the Supreme Court, he thinks four would be sufficient. The Chief Justice was of an age that rendered him incapable of active work. The associate Judge was not efficient. The three Puisne Judges were men of vigor and ability. They were Halliburton. Wilkins and Uniacke. His plan was to get Mr Blowers to resign, to pension off Mr. Wiswell, and make a new Puisne Judge. He proposed a salary of £800 to £1000 currency, for a Judge, and £1000 to £1200 for the Chief Justice. By thus reducing the numbers the expense would be little increased, while it would put the Court in a state of efficiency, and provide a fair remuneration for Judicial services. This scheme however, which he directed Sir. Peregrine to submit to the House, did not meet with the favor of that body, and therefore the Judicial salaries remained as they were. In the other dispatch, marked private, Lord Goderich goes into other matters connected with the Judiciary. As regards the Chief Justiceship he announces the decision he had come to, and desires Mr. Jeffrey to converse with Mr. Blowers, Mr. Halliburton and Mr. Archibald with perfect freedom on the whole subject. He says he would not have proposed Mr. Blowers retirement, had he not been assured it would be perfectly agreeable to him. He then goes on to say that Mr. Halliburton having so long executed the duties of Chief Justice, he considered he had a claim, impossible to overlook, to succeed to that office, while his doing so would open the only means of effecting a reduction of the number of Judges. He desired that Mr Archibald should be informed of the reasons by which he had been influenced. "I am anxious" he wrote, "that he should know that I appreciate his zealous efforts in His Majesty's service, and I acknowledge the strength of his claim on the Crown." He proceeded to state that until something more advantageous could be effected for him, he intended, if, as he anticipated, there should be the means of doing so, to make an addition to the salary of the Attorney General, which he did not at present consider suitable to the great importance of the office, more especially since certain changes in the mode of disposing of the Crown Lands had taken away a large amount of fees, formerly received from that department." No sooner had the propositions to the Assembly contained in the one Dispatch been rejected by that body, than the power conferred by the other was promptly acted upon. Mr. Jeffrey reports to the Colonial Minister that he has conversed freely with the Chief Justice with the Judge and with the Attorney General. He says that Mr. Blowers proposed to retire at once, and that thereupon he had appointed Mr. Halliburton Chief Justice. He assigns as a reason for his prompt action that otherwise there would have been no President of the Council. He forgets to say that when Mr. Blowers was Chief Justice he did not always attend the Council. That of late years he had attended only occasionally. That formerly for a considerable period, when Doctor Croke administered the Government, he abstained from attendance of set purpose, and yet all the while there was no difficulty about holding a council. There was no need to assign any reason for acting on Lord Goderich's Dispatch. To assign as a reason that which was no reason at all, creates the suspicion that the haste was due to a different cause altogether. It was evidently the object of the parties interested to make assurance doubly sure, by effecting a permanent arrangement while they had the power.

We have entered upon these details, we confess with some reluctance. No two men could probably be found in this Province at that day with a higher sense of personal honor, than the candidates for this high office. Neither would do an act that he considered low or mean. and yet we find them obilged to dangle about the antichamber of a Minister in Downing Street, like lacqueys, soliciting a place, with certificates of character and previous good behaviour. And yet such was a necessity of public life in the Colonies in those days. At all events any one who could not stoop to establish an interest in the Colonial Office, by being himself the advocate of his own claims, could not hope to arrive at the higher positions of official life. He might be returned to the House as a representative, he might have great weight in the Assembly and with the people, he might guide the current of Legislation, and be looked up to as a man of mark, but the gates of public office were closed to him. If that were his aim, he must forego the popular favor, creep into the Council, and abjure his liberal sentiments. After he had done all this, and made his peace with the Body he had joined, and quarrelled with the Body he had left, he might hope for the favor of the Crown. Few men had the courage to brave the Council and the Lieutenant Governor and go behind them, and establish a position with the Colonial Office. Indeed when they did take that step, they were open to the suspicion arising from a position so equivocal. When they secured the favor of the Minister, they were in danger of losing that of the people. If they retained popular support, and came into competition at the Colonial Office with those who were sustained by the local Government, the contest generally ended, as it did in this case, with victory to the nominee of the Council. On the whole, the proceeding was a forlorn hope. Few attempted it, and of these few a very limited number succeeded. Subserviance was a better pass-port than independence, to the favor of the Crown. In the end as a rule the favorite of the Council was the successful man. His path was easy and strewed with flowers. To be sure he had to abandon the popular branch, he had to hide himself within the closed doors of the Council Chamber. If it was a living entombment, at all events the mausoleum was gilded. The new convert had to breathe the spirit and cherish the ideas of an age that was past: he was to be a political anachronism—an official fossil, amid the changing and advancing forms of political thought.

The election of 1830 was followed by a great reaction, which began to show itself towards the close of the first session of the new House. The members, no longer united by a question appealing to their *esprit de corps*, broke up into parties according to their ordinary proclivities. Meanwhile the press was active in disseminating the principles of the liberal party. Mr. Howe who had now acquired experience as an editor was urging from day to day his advanced views on political subjects. These were becoming popular in the country, and in turn were reacting on the House. Towards the end of the term in the years 1835 and 1836, this spirit became more obvious. Mr. Doyle in his witty way said, that after six years of sin they had entered on a year of repentance. The House was prorogued in April 1837, and preparations were soon entered upon for a general election. This would have taken place earlier, but for the delay in obtaining the assent of the Crown to Bills for the division of some of the Counties, (Halifax among the number) and adding to their representation. This assent was not obtained till November. Thereupon the House was at once dissolved and writs were issued for a new election, returnable on the 12th of January following.

During the summer appeared a series of remark. able letters addressed to the freeholders of the Province over the signature of Joe Warner, in which the proceedings

of the last House were discussed with great vigor and
ability, by a writer evidently well versed in public affairs. The letters began in July and continued to the
very eve of the election. They were thirteen in number, and were directed largely against the lawyers, but
special attention was given to Mr. Archibald, who was
charged with a great variety of public offences, but principally with waste and extravagance in the Provincial
expenditure. These letters were extensively read in
every part of the Province, and doubtless contributed
largely to the excitement of the subsequent election.

In Mr. Archibald's county, being the one formerly
constituting the District of Colchester, only about fifty
electors out of the twelve hundred had been found, in
1830 to record their votes against him, but he was now
to find a great change in public opinion in his County.
There can be no question that he rendered great service to
Colchester in the long period of thirty years that he had
been in the Legislature, and might have looked, if any
public man is ever justified in looking, for the gratitude
of his constituents. But the leaven of the Nova Scotian
and of the Recorder had begun to permeate the masses
and to affect Mr. Archibalds' supporters. Mr. Isaac Logan
was pitched upon as the candidate to oppose him. Mr.
Logan was a resident of Onslow, having many years before removed from Cumberland, of which he was a native,
and settled in Colchester, where he married. He was a
man of fair abilities with a good common school education,
but had little knowledge of political matters beyond what
he gathered from the newspapers. He was an occasional
contributor to the *Nova Scotian* where certain articles
under the signature of L. give a fair, but certainly not
very high, idea of his political and educational attainments.

Mr. Logan was an Elder of the Presbyterian Church, and, through his marriage, was connected with a large and influential family in the County. From these various sources, the gathering in favor of Mr. Logan, though by no means formidable, was very much in excess of what Mr. Archibald could have anticipated. The election was held on the 28th November. Mr. Logan was requested. as the Junior candidate to speak first, but he declined. Then Mr. Archibald spoke, referring to the charges which had been spread broadcast over the County, in reference to his political conduct. Adverting to the commutation of the Quit Rents, he said :—

"Little did he expect that any man in the country who was relieved by that measure, from any claim of the King upon his land, would have raised his voice against him. He was aware that the Joe Warner of the *Recorder*, who was a second time discovered, by his eloquence of abuse, and who was in a minority on that occasion, would make wicked use of it. There were some in that minority whom he respected, but Joe Warner had advocated the measure of commutation, some five years previous, quite as strenuously as he, the Attorney General had done, and here he read a speech from the paper of that day. " But suppose when the representatives of the agricultural parts of the Province were desirous of settling the question, I had interposed and said with him, no, Let the King collect his own rents, and they had been collected, what would have been the complaint against me ? You sir, well knew that your office would have been enriched by the collection, and therefore you opposed the commutation, that yourself and the King's bailiffs, might come forth like a flight of destroying angels upon the country. With the disposition to libel me, no course of policy could have protected me. I did what I deemed right and proper, regardless of my enemies, and posterity will remember me with gratitude. But it is said my salary as an officer of the Crown was dependent on the measure, and likewise the arrears due me. I would ask if there is any man, who is fit to go abroad without a keeper, who could suppose that so essential an officer as the King's Attorney General would be left to seek his own salary. No, gentleman, when the Government fails to provide the means for paying such an officer, it will be near its dissolution. The arrears due me could not be paid from the casual revenue here, without a grant from Parliament to relieve it."

* * * * * *

The Attorney General then stated the many ties that bound him to his native country. He had been absent from it first for his education, and since, he had travelled far and seen many countries, but he always returned to it with increased affection. The constituency might separate him from it, but it would not be without a struggle, and one of no ordinary kind. It would be like the severance of a limb by violence from the living body. He had never disgraced them, and if once severed, it would be once and forever. But he knew the men of Colchester, and he confided in them. The best evidence of his confidence was that he solicited a vote from no man. Nay, he said that he hoped that if he could have the meanness to ask any one for his vote, that that man would have spirit enough to vote against him. I am regardless, continued the Attorney General, of a paper character, which like a kite must be kept up by the uncertain breeze, and balanced by the length of the train. I am likewise regardless of paper attacks upon a well earned reputation. I ask those who meet me in the walks of every day life to certify for my character. I ask the merchant, the mechanic, the grocer and every man with whom I deal; I ask the farmer who ploughs my field and reaps my harvest, and my domestic servants, whose wages have never been kept back. I ask those who are in distress, tribulation and poverty, the living compound mass of society to certify for me. I am proud to say that in the metropolis where I reside, I have received from all classes evidence of their esteem and kindness, and although I have been long absent from you, my name I am confident is not forgotten."

On the second day of the polling Mr. Logan, finding himself some four hundred behind, resigned the contest, and was about to leave the hustings, when Mr. Archibald asked him to remain, as he had something to say in which he was interested. After some preliminary remarks he proceeded to say :—

" Did the worthy candidate suppose that now the contest being ended he was to make his bow and retire. That he was to enter the field with me, attack my reputation, dearer to me than life, and when foiled and defeated, notwithstanding all the falsehood and fraud he has employed against me, that he was to walk away with, the mawkish leave he has taken of you, without the least notice from me.

*   *   *   *   *   *   *   *   *

Speaking of Joe Warner he said—against him he had advocated the cause of the early settlers of the country. He had sustained and defended, when they were slandered, the characters of the first teachers of religion in this Western World. Here he enumerated the names of the clergymen, now deceased, who he said had shared the privations and poverty of the Fathers of the present generation; men who were held up to scorn and derision by Mr. Logan's friend, Joe Warner, denounced as sectarians, disaffected to the Government and unworthy of confidence." Yet these were the men who first preached the gospel amongst you. These were they who spread a table in the wilderness and made the weary pilgrim drink from the ordinances of religion, as from a brook running in the way. These were they who shared the humble dwellings of the congregations committed to their charge; and when the angel of death visited their habitations, gave the cup of consolation to the mourner. These whom I have named are departed and gone to their everlasting reward. While living, I had their confidence, and now that they are dead, I revere their memory. Such men are not likely again to visit you. I will not enumerate the living who also claim my esteem, and whom it has been my pride likewise to defend against the common enemy, who is now combined with the Presbyterian interest to put me down, and place the pious Deacon in my stead. One I cannot refrain from mentioning, the Reverend Clergyman of this parish, Mr. Waddell. He is, as it were, between the living and the dead. It has pleased the Almighty to afflict him, and deprive you of his ministrations, but as I heard from a much respected friend, who occupied his place the last Sunday, you have the benefit of his prayers for you. His life has been a living sermon. His example is worthy of your imitation. He has not laboured for the meat that perisheth, for his labor did not even procure it for himself and his family. And if in the evening of his days he has parted with an earthly dwelling to release himself from embarrassment, he has secured a better inheritance: he has taken the Almighty for his refuge, and the most High for his habitation.

Once more I must mention the Rev. Dr. McCulloch, the man who first made science familiar to those, who without his aid must forever have remained in ignorance. Would that I possessed a tithe of those talents, which would have given him elevated rank in any other country. He also has been assailed by the man who now joins hands with the worthy candidate against me, and this opposition, strange to say, has risen among the Presbyterians, whom I have defended, and for whom I laboured to maintain an institution of learning, which their dissentions have destroyed, while my Baptist friends have been united in their cause and will prevail. They have had and shall have my support. I have done but my duty to worthy men whose acquaintance I am proud to have made, and whose confidence I have enjoyed, and but for the advice of one of them, whom I shall ever esteem ; but that he requested me to bridle my tongue on a subject pregnant of so much feeling, I would chastise the gentleman, and perhaps his associates, with a whip of scorpions, which they would remember to the end of their days. To him he is indebted for any mercy he may receive at my hands.

* * * * * * * * *

The worthy candidate has told you of his labours in electioneering, because he was not generally known throughout the country, which I promise shall not be his case hereafter. He has indeed been industrious. He has carried Joe Warner into the heart of every family. Even since my arrival in the County he has been favored with the 13th Epistle. Milton was contented to abuse the devil with only twelve books. Upon me, Joe Warner has bestowed the baker's dozen.   He established a co-partnership with his friend, Deacon Logan.   Joe was the manufacturer of slander and libel, and the worthy candidate became the hawker, the peddler, and the petty chapman of his wares.   I leave it to the strong distinguishing mind which he says he possesses, to establish any difference in guilt between them.   But no one could charge him with vending without license, and so successful was the deacon, that he created a demand for misrepresentation and falsehood, which even the diabolical skill, and wicked industry of Joe Warner himself could scarcely supply.   Indeed, he was so hard pressed that, on one occasion, he forgot his friend, the deacon, and nearly blasted his hopes, by recommending you' to return me. The worthy candidate, who is an agriculturist, in opposition to me, who have expended more among you, in one speculation for the benefit of the County, than he ever expended in his life, did not confine himself to the slow process of the drill culture with the seeds of Joe Warner. No, gentlemen, he scattered them with a liberal and diabolical broadcast over the whole face of the County, and his sowing for a time was not in vain.   The abominable seed took root.   The Hellebore and the Hemlock, the Cicuta and the Nightshade, sprang up in the footsteps of the deacon, and he had the hopes of an abundant harvest, but the noxious plants were blasted and scattered before their appointed time.   Would you believe it, that a man reported as pious, would send his messenger before him to the upright, the honest inhabitants of Earltown, and request them to assemble, as he was coming among them and had good news to bring.   Gentlemen, what were these good news.   What was the gospel, according to Isaac Logan ?   It was neither more nor less than a new sheaf of the manufactures of his friend. How beautiful upon those snowy mountains were the feet of the deacon, shod with the preparation of the *Acadian Recorder*, and heel-tapped with the lies of Joe Warner! The good news was to tell them, that the man who had maintained an unsullied reputation, the man who had hitherto enjoyed their confidence, was a villian. But he will find with all his outfit of iniquity, that he has walked with vanity, and his feet have hastened after deceit."

* * * * * * * * *

In reference to personal solicitation he said he denounced it. He put himself in the true sense of the ex pression upon the Country. He requested that if in the immense Assembly he was addressing, there was a man he had injured, he would rise and charge him, or if on the other hand there was one who had applied to him for relief and been dismissed, that he would stand up and accuse him. These he said were bold challenges, but he made them without fear.

* * * * * * * *

Gentlemen I am proud of your confidence. It has given the lie to my enemies, it has rivetted an attachment already strong, to my native county. I am shortly to return to the metropolis, to engage once more in the important duties of my office, but I will remember your kindness, and I know I shall not be forgotten by you. I shall feel more strongly than ever the desire which has grown with my labors, and increased upon me, when I have been in distant countries, of residing among you. And should I be spared to old age, I shall comfort myself with the hope, of spending a part at least of the evening of my days, beside that stream, on the banks of which in adversity my mother nursed me. My name shall remain and stand connected with Colchester, when the name of Joe Warner shall be rotten as his compost, and stink like his dung hill."

Nothing but the heat and passion of the moment while smarting under a sense of the injustice and malevolence of the charges brought against him, which had led so many of his old friends into the arms of the enemy, and the knowledge that Mr. Logan had been the main instrument in scattering these charges among the people, and seducing them from their old allegiance, could justify the fierceness of this invective.

It was perhaps the more inexcusable that Mr. Logan was no match for him, and there was none of Joe Warner's letters to suggest the answer to such an address. We doubt if Joe Warner himself could have stood much better the storm of fiery darts that shot with such rapidity from the quiver of the Attorney General. It was perhaps well that Mr. Logan was unable to answer. As he left the hustings after this scathing attack, his cowering form, and melancholy face, excited a commiseration which he could not have received if he had attempted a reply.

Mr. Logan returned to his home, if not cured of his ambition, at all events determined not to enter again on so unequal a contest.

CHAPTER VIII.

Curious results of Election. General effect of same. Disappearance of old members. First appearance of new men afterwards attaining eminence. Re-elected Speaker. Illness. Mr. Smith appointed Speaker temporarily. Failure of crops in 1836. Mr. Dodd brings a Bill before the House to keep grain and potatoes in the Province. Mr. Archibald's speech in its favor. Mr. Young opposes the measure. His death. Resolutions transmitted to England. Reply. Rebellion in Lower Canada. Troops sent from Halifax to Montreal. Public Meeting at Halifax. Resolutions for relief of Soldiers' families. Patriotic speech of Mr. Archibald. Mr. Howe's vindication of the loyalty of the Liberals of Nova Scotia. Meeting of House in 1838. Appointment of Lord Durham as Lord High Commissioner and Governor General of British North America. His Report on the situation of the Provinces. An act of his administration attacked in the Lords by Lords Brougham and Lyndhurst. The Ministry disallow the ordinances complained of. Lord Durham's hasty return to England. Lord John Russel becomes Colonial Secretary. Mr. C. Poulett Thompson appointed Governor General. Resolutions of 1839. Delegates sent by House to England. Met by Council's Delegates. Lord John Russell's despatch of 16th October, 1839, as to tenure of Office. Additions to Executive Council from Assembly. Vote of want of Confidence in Government. Resignation of Hon. J. B. Uniacke. Subsequent action of House. Vote against Sir Colin Campbell. Mr. Archibald's views on that vote. The Governor General at Halifax. Lord Falkland becomes Governor of Nova Scotia. New appointments to Council. Election of 1840. Mr. Archibald returned for Colchester without opposition.

When the battle of the general election was over, and the smoke had cleared away, some odd results were observed. Mr. John Young had, in the House, and in the press, constituted himself in a peculiar manner the champion of reform. He had spoken and written on the subject with great vehemence, and it might have been expected that his constituents would have received him with open arms, as the bold defender of the peoples rights. But when he went to his election, he found himself at the end of the second day's polling at Antigonish, the lowest on the list. He was 300 below Mr. McDougall, and, 100 below Mr. Wilkie; but Sydney was a Catholic County, and the Bishop was his friend. On the third morning of the polling, His Lordship appeared on the hustings and called on his people to rally round Mr. Young. The result, was that that gentleman at the close of the Poll, though continuing to hold the same relation as before to Mr. McDougall, had a majority of thirty over Mr. Wilkie.

On the other hand, Mr. Archibald had gone to a County in which, perhaps as much as in any other part of the Province, the new doctrines had taken root,—he had to labor against the prejudices created by changes,—some unjust, some perhaps not altogether without foundation, and yet such was the fascination of his manner and such his powers of persuasion, when brought face to face with the people, that he was returned by a triumphant majority. It must have been a double mortification to Mr. Young, first, to see the man who was his principal object of attack, swept into the Assembly on the very crest of the popular wave, and secondly, to find himself the friend of the people, saved from political extinction, only by a Bishop. Upon the whole however, a great change had swept over the representation of the country. When the House met on the 31st of January, many faces were there which the chamber had never seen before. Many faces once familiar to it had disappeared from the scene. Of the old members, Archibald and Uniacke, Stewart and Doyle, Young and Huntingdon, were the leading men returned. But where was Lawson whose well known form had flitted across the floor for the last thirty-one years, and was almost a pillar of the House? Where was Roach of Annapolis, the acrid and acid opponent of the legal profession, the author of cheap Law

Bills, and the most vehement of sticklers for extreme reform ? He had disappeared and was no more seen. Where was Dickson of Pictou who for nearly twenty years had been a member, whose handsome face and manly figure were familiar to all frequenters of the Assembly, and who had been in his quiet way a power in former Houses ? The place that erst knew him, now knew him no more,' at least for a season. Where were DeBlois of Halifax and Morse of Amherst, Creighton of Lunenburgh, and DeWolf of Windsor, all men of mark in their time? Gone. Gone. But we need not pursue our political obituary. Of the men now assembled, over thirty had never sat in the House before. Many of them afterwards, achieved distinction in public life. Mr. Howe at this session commenced a Legislative career, which terminated with the office of Governor, held by him at the time of his death. Mr. W. Young was afterwards to be Chief Justice.* Mr. DesBarres and Mr. Dodd to be Judges of the land. Mr. McDougall was to be a Solicitor General. Mr. DeWolf and Mr. S. P. Fairbanks to hold important departmental positions, and Mr. Annand, who is still living in England, was to be premier of the Province, and for a number of years to exercise a large amount of political power. All these came into the Assembly in 1837. When the House met, Mr. Archibald was again unanimously chosen as speaker. But he had only to look round the red benches, and notice the faces of the new men seated there, to be satisfied that the period of his ascendency was coming to a close. The work to be done, if these men were to determine its character, must be

---

* Mr. Young had indeed been returned in 1833 but had sat only part of a session, being unseated on the petition of Richard Smith who took his place, and therefore he may be said to have been first a member in 1837.

much more thorough and radical than would suit his political proclivities. He seems indeed to have taken little part in the debates of the first session, and hardly any in the stormy discussion connected with the passing of Mr. Howes' twelve celebrated resolutions. Indeed his health had begun to yield to the pressure upon energies seriously taxed by the labors of a life time. An entry on the Journals the 3rd April, 1837, after the House had been two months in session, recalls the memory of an event which at the time excited a great sensation. When the members met on Monday morning Mr. Archibald was not in the chair. The Clerk rose and informed them that the Speaker had desired him to say he was unwell and unable to attend the House that day, but that he hoped to do so in a few days. The Members adjourned till next morning. When they met again a resolution was adopted, referring to the illness of Mr. Archibald, and describing it as dangerous, and declaring the necessity of electing a temporary Speaker. Mr. George Smith, his old colleague in the representation of Halifax County, was put in the chair, till Mr. Archibald should recover. His illness was stated in the newspapers to be an attack of erysipelas in the face. It was really a severe stroke of paralysis. He had had a light attack of the kind, some years before when travelling on the continent of Europe, but he had recovered rapidly, and seemed to have suffered no ill effects from it, but this attack was more serious. It was some time before he began to rally, and even when he had recovered sufficiently to appear in public, it was seen that the blow had left its mark behind. The usual nervous consequences of this illness were perceptible in his face, and in his utterance. He never entirely recovered from the effects in either respect. However when the House met again in the beginning of 1838, after the prorogation, he was able to resume the chair, and to discharge with grace and dignity the duties which long usage had rendered easy. From this period however, till the close of his life, he was careful to avoid excitement. Indeed from the state of his health, he could not have longer continued, even if the Assembly had been composed of different materials, to take the leading part he had formerly done in the discussions of the House.

Another matter of local importance occasioned some discussion in the session of 1837. The previous season had been a bad one. Wet and cold had prevailed. The crops of potatoes were deficient in quantity, inferior in quality, and an early frost had cut off the crop before it was ripe. Oats, too, had been a failure. Petitions from every quarter for measures of relief were presented to the House. At length, Mr. Dodd introduced a Bill to prevent the exportation of grain and potatoes, and when this Bill went into Committee there were serious differences of opinion about the policy of passing it. Some members contended that the matter should be left to the operation of supply and demand. They thought the Bill a violation of the principles of political economy, that it was an imposition on the holders of the articles to which the prohibition would extend; that if relief was given at all, it should be in the shape of money from the Provincial Treasury. Mr. Archibald took an active part in the discussion, and we subjoin a few extracts from one of his speeches, to show the style of his opinions on such questions. Possibly his expressions may have been a little accentuated by the circumstance, that the writer of Joe Warner's letters took his stand against the Bill, on the principles of political economy. The Speaker

said : " It was not a new measure, either in this Province or in Great Britain, but it was one which should be
resorted to only in cases of great distress,—whether the
present juncture was of that nature, was the question for
the House now to determine. If gentlemen would undertake to say,—meddle not with the ordinary course of
things, allow the man who has the articles here to carry
them abroad, because there is distress in the other colonies, he would ask them what remedy they afforded,
when they turned round to the destitute and gave them
money ? It was the necessaries of life which were wanted, and they only would relieve the wants which were
now felt all over the country.

We had this year the appearance of a favorable
spring, and if we could argue anything from the present
weather, we might look forward to a fruitful season, but
what was the state of the country in regard to seed ? It
had none. In vain then were a genial atmosphere, and
an early season for the labors of the husbandman. The
unfortunate man who had not seed, would be obliged
to look forward to the extinction of all his hopes, to
years of famine and distress.—" And yet," continued the
Speaker, "when I make these statements I am to be met
with doctrines drawn from Adam Smith, my sympathies
are to be stifled, and my energies paralysed by the principles of political economy. I am to be told that I am
ignorant and understand not the subject. Mr. Chairman,
if I could sit down to a cold blooded speculation of the
misery of my fellow countrymen, if I could answer the
groans wrung from them by the hands of famine, by referring to the doctrines of philosophical speculators, then
perhaps I might appreciate, the arguments of the Hon.
Gentleman from the County of Sydney, but while I have

eyes to see and a heart to feel for the distress of the
country, I shall do all I can to extend the aid of the
Legislature to the relief of that distress, and shall willingly be considered ignorant, if to afford relief to suffering humanity, constitutes ignorance. Sir, this is the
country in which I hope to spend the remainder of my
days, and all the warmest feelings of my heart are en-
twined with its interests and prosperity. From one end
of the land to the other we hear re-echoed the cry of
scarcity, and we are called upon to extend our protection.
If in anticipating advantage from the present measure
we should find ourselves mistaken, it will be a satisfaction to have erred on the side of humanity. Are we to
be told that we are never to legislate in opposition to
certain laws and rules, which have been established by
political theorists. For what use then are we here?
Every law we pass is at variance from those principles
by which our conduct would otherwise be governed. If
there are men of minds so amazingly strong, that they
are able to lay down fixed principles, which are to be
applied, like the square and the rule, to every variety of
human exigencies, then indeed is a Legislature of no use.
But, Sir, the office and duty which we sustain are of a
higher order, we are to look at the present situation of
the country, and when our ears are saluted on all sides
with the cries of distress, we are to afford such practical
relief as our judgments suggest.

    *   *   *   *   *   *   *   *   *

With respect to the oatmeal, I may tell the Hon.
gentleman, that while others were writing about it and
talking about it, I was spending my money in endeavor-
ing to introduce the use of that article into the country.
I challenge any man to shew an equal amount of expense

incurred in an attempt to encourage the domestic manufactures of the country. I am therefore no theoretical speculator on possibilities. I have been practically engaged in trying an experiment in this branch of industry at my own risk, and asking not the aid of others. It is true that I have not been repaid my expenditure, but the country has been benefitted by it, and I reap the satisfaction of having done all I could for the encouragement of domestic manufactures.

* * * * * * * * *

Sir, it has been the will of Heaven to visit this country with a season worse than any we have had for a series of years, and the hopes and prospects of many, were withered by the untimely frost, which cut off many of the potatoes last year. Those which remained from that visitation have been almost unfit for consumption, and will scarcely answer for the purposes of seed. When then there is an extraordinary deficiency in every part of the country, when, from one end of the Province to the other, the cry of destitution resounds, shall we allow the only means of relief to be shipped from our ports without interposing a prohibition? I hope, however, our exertions will not stop here. I trust that before the House breaks up, they will put it in the power of the Government to purchase a sufficiency of seed to supply all who are unable to purchase for themselves. But, as a necessary preliminary measure we must take care that the seed does not go out of the country. It is in vain to taunt the distressed with a want of industry and application, it is not the want of industry as suggested by an Hon. gentleman, but the misery arising from causes over which the inhabitants of this country had no control, it was one of those dispensations of Heaven which are beyond the foresight of man. It is not in man to ensure success by his industry. The Hon. gentleman has no doubt read, " that the husbandman may nourish his plant in the morning, and make his seed to flourish in the evening, but the harvest notwithstanding becomes a heap in the day of distress and of bitter sorrow." We are called upon for relief, and shall we teach the applicants a lesson of economy at the expense of their lives. This very visitation, (and it is the way that Heaven deals with man) will have the effect of producing more good than all the lectures that could be given."

Mr. Young in his reply vindicates, with much force and eloquence, the views he had thrown out in his previous speech. Towards the close of his observations, he said " that he expected from the tone the Speaker had taken towards the conclusion of his address, that he was going to depart from the subject strictly before the House. He was glad he had not done so, on the present occasion. When he chooses to make the personal attack he had threatened, he (Mr. Y.) would be ready in his place to answer.

The threat to which Mr. Young refers is not contained in the reported speech, but it was well known that it was Mr. Archibald's intention ever since Joe Warner had held him up to public reprobation to square the account on the floor of the House, when the proper opportunity occurred. Some hint of the kind had probably dropped in the speech which Mr. Young was now answering, but if so, it seems to have escaped the notice of the reporter. A field day devoted to the points in difference between these two eminent men, would have enriched the debates of the session, but it was never to come off. The speeches above referred to were made on the

29th of March.   Five days afterwards, an event occurred which we have already narrated, that disabled Mr.
Archibald from carrying out his intention for the session,
and before the House met again, Mr. Young was no more,
having died an the 8th day of October, 1837, in the 65th
year of his age.

The Resolutions moved by Mr. Howe, and adopted
by the Assembly in 1837, were duly transmitted to England, and elicited voluminous replies from Lord Glenelg,
who then held the seals of the Colonial Office.   Every
disposition was shewn, on the part of the Imperial authorities, to meet the reasonable wishes of the Province, but
Sir Colin Campbell, the Lieutenant Governor, was not a
man to shake himself free from the trammels of his poli-
ical advisers, and little or nothing was done in the way
of concession to the Assembly's demands.

While these things were going on in Nova Scotia,
events were occurring in other British American Provinces, which, in their issue, affected the affairs of this
country.   Lower Canada had a population alien in creed,
in language, and in nationality, to that of the rest of British North America.   They were jealous of the rights conferred upon them by the Act, 14 Geo. III., commonly
called the Quebec Act. and were little disposed to support
administrations, largely English in feeling— and composed, as they considered, of an undue proportion of that
nationality.   They were also little accustomed to the free
institutions to which Englishmen are trained, and very
naturally carried to excess the liberties which, in their
new condition, devolved upon them.   It is not to be wondered at that, under such circumstances, the advocates of
reform in Lower Canada soon passed the boundary of
Constitutional agitation, and that they were looked upon

by men attached to the English connexion, as little better
than rebels in disguise. They soon took steps which
made them rebels undisguised. That they labored under
many and serious grievances, nobody now denies, but, the
moment they sought redress by unconstitutional means,
they lost the sympathy of their fellow colonists, suffering under similar conditions. Warrants were issued
against the more violent agitators, including some members of the Assembly. The parties concerned resisted
arrest and all of a sudden a rebellion ensued. Troops
were sent for from all quarters. Those at Halifax were
despatched to Montreal. In a few weeks the rebellion
was over, the prominent leaders either in prison, or in
exile. After the troops left Halifax, a public meeting
was called on the 3rd of December, 1837, at which resolutions were passed, deploring the events that had taken
place in Lower Canada, asserting the loyalty of the people of Nova Scotia of every class, and providing for the
raising of contributions for the wives and families of the
soldiers called away for the suppression of the rebellion.
This meeting was convened by the Sheriff, on a requisition signed by people of all classes. High Tories and
extreme Radicals alike took part in the demonstration.
The resolutions were passed unanimously. Mr. Archibald introduced them in a speech of some length of which
we shall quote a few extracts.

"I am happy to see so large and respectable a meeting of the inhabitants of the town called for the objects
stated in the requisition. The general scope of that requisition is, that, while deploring the situation of our fellow subjects in Lower Canada, it becomes us, who enjoy
the blessings of the British Constitution in peace, to de-
clare our firm devotedness to that constitution and also

to express a disposition to make provision for the wives
and children of those soldiers who have been moved so
unexpectedly from among us. Under that requisition
this large meeting of those who feel deeply interested
inthe country, is convened; disposed, no doubt, to support the objects specified. I have been absent from town,
and am therefore less acquainted than others with late
occurrences. This morning the Committee, which was appointed to draw up resolutions to be submitted to the
meeting, did me the honor to request me to propose those
resolutions. I come cheerfully to do so without preparation. Preparation is not requisite on the topic of these
resolutions. I will merely state the various subjects
which they embrace, and will then read them, when they
may either be passed separately or together as the meeting may see fit. Politics need not to be introduced at
this meeting: we have nothing to do with them: we look
round at the state of others, and sympathise with them,
while we ourselves enjoy the comforts of peace and safety. Although the loyalty of a people is generally to be
taken as a reasonable presumption, yet there are times
when it peculiarly becomes the duty of every man to de-
clare his sentiments, that those, who expect anything
else but true loyalty, may be undeceived, and may be convinced that they have been mistaken. I feel obliged to
the Committee who have placed these resolutions in my
hands. I am not disposed to put myself forward in public matters and I believe that this is the first Town
meeting which I have attended. I will make a few remarks on these resolutions and hope that they will be
passed without difficulty. Nothing will be found in them
which will compromise any principle.

The first resolution is intended to express the regret of

the meeting on the unfortunate state of affairs in Canada.
Whatever causes have produced these evils, acts of law-
less agression, which all must regret, have been committed. We are not here to try out all the particulars which
have led to this state. Now, we see an arm raised against
the law, and the government of the country, and every
one must lament this, and the devastation which ensues.
The resolution goes a little farther, and says that at this
time it becomes our duty to state our unshaken loyalty to
the Government under which we live, and that we are
disposed, one and all, to resist any attempt at severing this
Province from the Crown of Great Britain. I am proud
to see such a resolution as this considered in a meeting
of this kind. We will have no hesitation in declaring the
severance alluded to ruinous, and that we will do all we
can to prevent such a calamity.

The second resolution has reference to the removal
of the military. His Excellency the Lieutenant Governor acting with his usual promptness in military matters,
immediately, when circumstances required it, put orders
in requisition by which the troops which have been residing among us, deeming they were settled in their
homes at least for the winter, have been removed, and
have been sent to a scene of much toil and danger. This
resolution states the regret that is felt at the causes that
led to the removal. While here, the officers and men
made themselves esteemed and respected by the various
classes in the community : this will not be denied. There
are times when a few may express the public feeling,
and such occurs when a regiment is about leaving the
place of its temporary abode, but now, at this meeting,
which may be said to represent the Province, to pass a
compliment, such as that intended, would be an expression

of more than usual interest and weight. The resolution declares the highest esteem entertained for the officers and men who have been removed. This will doubtless be responded to unanimously. We will be proud of an opportunity of shewing to all, the sense we entertain of their services, the gratitude we feel, and the regret that their connexion with us has been so unexpectedly severed. We may thus follow them with kind wishes and our opinion of their conduct. This is the intent and substance of the second resolution. (Applause).

The third resolution commends itself to our best feelings—we are subjects of the Crown enjoying peace and quietness under the constitution, and we look to others less favorably circumstanced—we see the soldier taken from his home leaving his wife and family behind, destitute of their wonted support and protection. Altho' the spirit which animates the soldier is sufficient to make him face any hardship; altho' he may think but little of his journey thro' the winter wilderness, and of the dangers which await him at the end of it; altho' the call of duty is enough for these difficulties, has he not the feelings of a father and a husband for those from whom he is removed?

The removal of a civilian is different. He has time for preparation, and his family sinks into the ranks of society and are provided for. But when the soldier is thus removed, the usual support of his family is suddenly taken away, and feelings on such subjects must operate powerfully on the bravest men. He may think that he has to leave them in a country of strangers, but let us tell him that he leaves them among Englishmen. (Applause).

The object of this resolution is to state that we will

make provision for those who have been left behind, that as we have not been called to leave home under arms, as the soldiers have been—perhaps for our ultimate safety—we will assist in making those comfortable who remain, and in relieving the minds of those who have been forced to leave them comparatively destitute. I hope that none will feel disinclined to come forward in furtherance of this resolution, to express their esteem for those removed from us, and to assist in alleviating the sufferings of those whom our humanity can reach, the families which remain.

 * * * * * * *

Without dwelling on particulars any longer we may take the general scope of the resolution and see if it is not wise as regards the Government, the Canadian Provinces, and New Brunswick, as well as our own character, to make these declarations. By these, if any say, as has been said, not here, but elsewhere, that we wish to throw off our allegiance, we deny the imputation and say that it is grossly untrue. There is not a word of truth in such a charge. Loyalty is the characteristic of the Province of Nova Scotia. I am proud that the Committee called on me this day, not as an officer of the Crown, but as one placed at the head of the Assembly of the Province. I justly take a pride in having held that post for years, although an officer of the Crown, and I cannot allow any man to speak more confidently of the country than myself. Many of the inhabitants of the Province are descendents of those who took the wilderness as their portion, rather thangive up the British Constitution—all of them are proud of their descent, and their birth, and if the sentiments here expressed could be responded to, they would be echoed from every mountain and valley, and from every hamlet in the land. (Loud applause.)

The inhabitants of the land are loyal to a man, and no differences exist, except those for which proper and legal modes of redress are sought. We are, loyal people, and he who says the reverse, libels the Province, and says that which is untrue."

Mr. Howe afterwards spoke with much force and vigor. He said he had been stigmatised as "the Nova Scotian Papineau," and therefore claimed a right to explain how far his political sentiments were in accord with those of the French agitator. He said "I came here not only to express loyalty to Her Majesty, (and Heaven knows the Queen has not more loyal subjects in the same number in any part of her dominions than she has in Nova Scotia)—I came here not only to express my loyalty, but also to vindicate my public conduct and that of those with whom I have acted; to prove that never for a single moment did we harbor a thought which might not be spoken in the presence of the Queen."

The unanimity and enthusiasm of the meeting showed that, however much the Nova Scotian Liberals might differ from their Conservative brethren in questions of Reform, that both were of one mind as to the limits within which reform was to be sought. As Liberals, they had no idea of resorting to rebellion to obtain redress of any grievances they may have labored under.

The General Assembly was summoned for the twenty-fifth day of January, A. D. 1838. When they met it was at once felt that the time was inopportune for pressing their views on the Imperial Government, and accordingly little was done in the Assembly beyond discussing the answers given by the Crown in respect of the different subjects that had been brought to its notice. But while our Legislature was comparatively quiet, discussions were taking place in the Imperial Parliament which affected materially the future of all the Provinces. The Rebellion in Canada was too serious a matter to pass unnoticed. That country, it was admitted, labored under some real grievances, and the Ministry felt that the time had come when the facts should be investigated by some Imperial authority, capable of dealing with the question in a competent manner. All eyes turned to a statesman who had already achieved a high reputation in Parliament, and who seemed particularly fitted for the duty of the moment. Lord Durham was a man of great ability, he had held a prominent place in the politics of the Mother Country, from a time anterior to the Reform Bill of 1830. He had himself some share in the framing of that Bill, and was connected by family and political ties with Earl Grey, under whose administration that Bill had passed. Lord Durham was a warm supporter of his father in law. When Melbourne took the place of Grey, Lord Durham continued to occupy a proud place in politics, but his peremptory temper, and advanced views, made him anything but an agreeable colleague for the moderate Whigs, of whom Lord Melbourne was the chief. He was accordingly sent away as Ambassador to Russia, first in 1833, and again in 1835. He remained at St. Petersburg till just before the occurrence of the events in Lower Canada, which we have narrated. On his return to England he was selected for the work which the Government had before them in British North America. He was made Lord High Commissioner and Governor-General of the Canadas, and armed with the largest powers the Crown could confer, so as to be able to deal effectually with the Canadian question. He brought with him as secretaries two men of mark in English political life. He arrived at Quebec on the 27th May, 1838, and immediately set himself to the task of investigation, which lay before him. His labors resulted in a long and able report, embracing the whole question of the Government of the British North American Provinces, tracing to their sources the difficulties that had arisen, and embodying the policy with regard to the future, which he recommended to the Government of England. No State document that exists, has had so powerful an influence in the administration of the Colonies as this report of Lord Durham, though it was ushered into the world under most inauspicious circumstances. Before it was published—indeed, almost before it was put into shape—Lord Durham had petulantly resigned his post, and without waiting for the leave of the Crown, or communicating his intentions to the Ministry, was on his way to England to take his place in the House of Lords. In that House the difficulty had arisen which occasioned his sudden return. Lords Brougham and Lyndhurst had both been Chancellors, the first in a Liberal, the second in a Conservative administration. They had long been foes, but now both were out of office and leagued against the Government. Lord Brougham's exclusion by his own political friends, naturally soured him with Lord Melbourne's administration. He had been left out, though he had been Lord Chancellor first in Grey's administration and again in Melbourne's first Cabinet. His exclusion, therefore, was a personal indignity, to be repaid when the opportunity occurred. Brougham and Lyndhurst were the best speakers in the House of Lords. Both disliked Lord Durham, whose temper was bad, and who, in his encounters with these Lords, had inflicted severe wounds that were still rankling, when the opportunity of revenge turned up. They attacked Lord Durham with great bitterness. In truth, there were fair grounds for assault. The Governor-General had found, when he arrived at Quebec, a number of political prisoners on his hands, and did not know what to do with them. They could not be let loose in the community without danger to the public peace. They could not he punished without increasing the irritation, which it was Lord Durham's policy to allay. At length he decided to banish them to Bermuda. This was certainly an excess of power, and Lord Durham's special foes in the House of Lords charged the Ministry with being parties to the act, which they described as one of despotism, gross enough for a Russian autocrat. Unfortunately the Ministry was weak in debating power in the Lords. They defended the Governor-General feebly. At length, finding the feeling strong against them, they threw him over altogether. They sent out a dispatch, disallowing the ordinances to which objections had been made. This document crossed Lord Durham on his passage home. He had heard of the discussion and of the course of Ministers in the Upper House, through an American newspaper, and forthwith, in his impetuous way, threw up his office. Disgusted and disheartened by the treatment of his friends, and suffering from the pressure of excessive labor, with failing health, Lord Durham did not long survive his return to England.

His Report was published in January 1839. It was felt to be a masterly production. It pointed out the policy to be pursued in the future with great force and persuasiveness.

In this year Lord John Russel became Colonial Secretary, in place of Lord Normanby who had held the seals of the office for a few months, in succession to Lord Glenleg, who was in office when the Ministry was form- ed. Lord John entered upon the duties of the Depart- ment with great vigor. One of his first acts was to select a disciple and friend of Lord Durham to succeed him in the office which that nobleman had so suddenly vacated. Mr. C. Poulett Thompson, afterwards Lord Sydenham, ar- rived at Quebec on the 19th of October. Soon after- wards he received copious instructions from the new Colonial Secretary.

In the session of 1839, the subject embraced by Mr. Howe's twelve resolutions was again brought before the House, and another series of resolutions adopted by a large majority. One of these provided that delegates should be sent to England to press upon the Imperial authorities the reform demanded by the House. In these proceedings Mr. Archibald, as we have said, had taken no conspicuous part. The House was then under the lead- ership of Mr. Howe, whose views on the subject, were much in advance of those held by the Speaker. Still, when the time came for appointing the delegates, Mr. Archibald's name was the first mentioned by Mr. Howe for that office. The Speaker however, courteously but firmly declined. He put his refusal on the ground of his position as head of the House, but it cannot be doubted that the feeling to which we have alluded, of his not be- ing able to enter with zeal on the task of promoting views with which he did not fully sympathize, had much to do with the determination at which he had arrived. When the question lay between the Representatives of the peo- ple and the nominees of the Crown, when it was disputed whether taxation should be imposed by men who enjoyed, or by those who did not enjoy, the confidence of the people, Mr. Archibald had no doubt or misgivings. But he had been bred to great reverence for the constituted authorities of the Empire—he had a profound respect for the doctrines on which the constitution of the Province was based, and finding the country prospering, notwithstanding the political difficulties, under a kind of government, which was now over a century old, he was hardly prepared for the extreme changes, advocated by the popular party, and did not care to undertake a mission to which he could give only a half hearted support. Be that as it may, the choice of the House next fell on Mr. W.Young and Mr. Huntingdon, who proceeded early in the summer to England, and entered at once into communication with the Imperial authorities, on the various subjects embraced in the resolutions of the House. They were met at the Colonial Office by two members of the Legislative Council who had been sent by that body to uphold the views of the minority in the Assembly. The Ministers of the Crown had thus the opportunity of hearing both sides of the question. They heard the opinions of the majority of the Assembly criticised by men of the standing and ability of Mr. Stewart of Amherst, and Mr. Wilkins of Windsor. Lord Normanby held the seals of the Colonial Office at the time, and in the course of the summer forwarded to the Lieutenant Governor of Nova Scotia despatches relative to the subjects embraced in the resolutions. But in September a change took place in the British Ministry. Lord Normanby went to the Home Office, and his position at the head of the Colonial Office, was filled by Lord John Russell who soon signalized his advent to the Department by acts of a bolder and more vigorous character than those of his predecessor.

Mr. Poulett Thompson (afterwards Lord Syden-

ham) had been sent out as Governor General, at a time
when the affairs of the two Canadas were becoming extremely critical, and Lord John furnished him with a
letter and copious instructions to guide him in the discharge of his duties.   These were dated the 14th October
1839, and two days later the Minister addresses a circu-
lar to all the Governors of the British North American
Colonies, dated the 16th October 1839.   This more than
any other state paper of the century, except Lord
Durham's celebrated Report, has become famous in the
annals of these Provinces.   In it Lord John Russell lays
down certain ruels, thereafter to be in force, as regards
the tenure of office.   He declares, in most emphatic
terms, that offices are no longer to held for life—That all
officers will be expected to retire from the public service
as often as any sufficient motives of public policy may
suggest the expediency of that measure—and that a
change in the person of the Governor, would be consider
ed a sufficient reason for any alterations which his suc-
cessor might deem it expedient to make in the list of
public functionaries.   The new policy was not to extend
to Ministerial or Judical offices, but was to be applicable in
a special manner to Heads of Departments.   This despatch
was the first of the two to be made public.   Some time
afterwards the previous Despatch of the 14th October, to
the Governor General, was published.   This was much
more guarded in its language, and really was not altogether consistent in tone and expression with the circu-
lar issued two days later.   The difference between the
two document was afterwards seized upon as a ground
for not acting on the latter despatch·   The difference
in language might reasonably have created some hesi-
tancy on the part of a Governor, not himself a States-

man, and surrounded by astute ministers, whose interests and prejudices were all in the line of opposition to
the concessions which the despatch was supposed to
yield. Sir. Colin it is true, did take some steps to introduce new material into his Executive Council. Mr.
James B. Uniacke. Mr. Dodd and Mr. DeWolf from the
House of Assembly were added to that body, but unfortunately the selection was not from the party of the
majority, but from that of the minority, in the Assembly.
While therefor the policy of the Imperial Government
was to harmonize the two parties by adding to the exist-
ing members of Council new men, drawn from the Assembly, enjoying the confidence of the people—the act of Sir.
Colin only added to the Council, persons of the same
modes of thought, and left the sentiment of the great
majority of the Assembly wholly unrepresented. The
result of such a proceeding might easily have been fore-
seen. The great majority of the Assembly who had carried the resolutions, felt themselves insulted by the
studious exclusion of every member of their party from
the new additions to the Council. When the House met
in 1840 they soon proceeded to express their feelings.
They passed resolutions by an immense majority stating
their grievances and wound up with the declaration
" that the Council as at present constituted did not pos-
ses the confidence of the House." When this resolution
passed, Mr. James B. Uniacke, a member of the Government, who had in 1830 succeeded to the seat vacated by
his brother Richard, on his promotion to the Bench, and
had ever since been the Champion of the Legislative
Council in the contest with the Assembly, bowed to the
decision of the House and resigned his seat in the Cabinet.
The House sent their resolution to the Governor and in

return received a reply, stating that the questions embraced in the resolution had already been submitted to the Imperial authorities, whose decision on the several subjects had been recently communicated to the House in Despatches he had directed to be laid on their table. The Depatches so referred to were those of the Marquis of Normanby, but no allusion was made to the later Despatches of Lord John Russel the then Colonial Secretary.

The House were naturally indignant at being referred to documents of August, emanating from a minister who had ceased to be the head of the Department, when no notice was taken of those of the 14th and 16th October, written and transmitted by the gentleman then holding the seals of the Colonial Office. This irritation was not lessened by an observation contained in the reply of Sir Colin Campbell, that he had no reason to believe the views of Ministers had undergone any change. They accordingly proceeded to pass an address calling the Governor's attention to Lord John's despatches; but their hopes of obtaining any concession were extinguished by Sir Colin's reply, "that if he adopted the views of the Assembly, he would recognize a fundamental change in the constitution of the Province—a step of too serious a character to take without first consulting the Imperial authorities on the subject." There was doubtless some ground for the hesitation of Sir Colin—but the Assembly having been baffled in their views ever since 1837, felt that the time had come when they must either recede from their demand, or ask the Sovereign to remove her representative, and send in his place another who would carry out the policy to which the English ministry were committed. It was a strong measure to take, it was one

at which many of the more moderate members of the
Assembly revolted. Outside of political matters, Sir Colin
was well liked. He was courteous and genial in manner,
a brave soldier, and exemplary in all the relations of
private life. Still the majority saw no other way of carrying their point. Hitherto they had treated Sir Colin
as a governor, guided by responsible advisers, and had
charged on them the shortcomings of which they complained, but, after a warm and heated discussion, they
now passed an address to the Crown, (which however
they had the good feeling not to ask him to transmit),
praying for his removal, and for the appointment of some
one who would carry out the policy of the Imperial authorities. This address was to be transmitted to the
Colonial Office through the head of the House. In this
proceeding Mr. Archibald seems to have taken no part.
His position as Speaker confined him to the chair, and
there is nothing in the Journals, or in the Press of the
day, to indicate the views he held on the final resolution,
bearing on the removal of the Lieutenant Governor. He
must have felt this to be a cruel stigma upon Sir Colin,
and it was one which Mr. Archibald from the natural
kindness of his feelings and his gentle temper, would be
most unwilling to inflict. His real views we gather from
a letter to Sir Colin, which appeared some time afterwards among the papers submitted to the Imperial Parliament. It seems Sir Colin had asked him for his official
opinion as Attorney General, on the Despatches, and in
reply, after stating, that, as the head of the Assembly,
it would not be proper for him to oppose the wishes of
that body, as expressed by their resolution, still he felt
that Sir Colin had a right to his opinion as principal officer of the Crown. He admitted there was room for

doubt whether the Despatches would bear the construction put upon them by the House. He considered the
Governor had acted prudently in awaiting further instruction before taking final action. There was one point
in the matter which had an important bearing. The Executive Council was a Court of Appeal, and had other
Judicial functions devolving upon it by law. The members of this Council had been appointed and still held
their commissions. It might give rise to doubt in legal
proceedings, how far that Council could be swept away,
and a new one put in its place, without the express authority of the Crown. The Royal instructions gave power
in certain contingencies to suspend a particular council-
lor, but there was no authority to deal with them as a
body; and, on the whole, with the doubts, that hung over
the construction of the Despatches, he could not but consider the course adopted by Sir Colin in his proposal to
submit the whole matter to the Ministers, as a prudent
and proper course. so long as any doubt rested on his
mind on the subject.

It is quite obvious from this letter how far the opinions of the majority of the House, had outrun those of
its Head. It is easy to see also that henceforth a greater
divergency would arise. His increasing age, for he was
now over sixty three years old, and his declining health,
pointed out to him that the time had arrived, in which
he was no longer to be the leading champion of popular rights, and in which he might gracefully fold his
cloak about him and retire from a scene, the actors in
which had undergone such changes. A Poetaster of the
day gives the characters and opinions of the different
members of the House in language, which if not very refined, at all events serves to show the general notion

entertained by the members of the majority, of the opinions and characters of the different members. The verses on the Speaker indicate the doubts which were entertained of his loyalty to the pronounced opinions of Mr. Howe's party in the Assembly.

The Speaker

> " Up ambitious steep you go
> While party strife divides the throng
> And few pretend to guess or know,
> To which side you belong.

> " You were the people's strong defence
> When Councillor's their rights 'assailed ;
> Your talents, genius, eloquence,
> O'er Tory power prevailed."

The Resolution for Sir Colin's removal was carried by a large majority, but some members who had voted for the other resolutions, declined to become parties to what had the appearance of a personal attack. The address was forwarded to the Colonial authorities through the Speaker, and a copy handed to the Lieutenant Governor. In the course of the summer Mr. Thompson, the Governor General, came to Halifax, assumed the reins of Government, and spent a week discussing with the leading men of both parties the difficulties of the situation. He appears to have impressed those with whom he communicated with the necessity of making mutual concessions. In a few months the result of the address and of the interviews and discussions with the Governor General appeared. Lord Falkland was sent out in September, to replace Sir Colin Campbell, and, on the 3rd October, five of the old members of the Executive Council sent in their resignations. On the 6th, three members of the Assembly, selected by the Colonial Office were appointed, under instruction, in their place.

Of these, the first was Mr. Archibald, whose moderation had probably recommended him for the position. The second was Mr. J. B. Uniacke who though he now sided with the majority, was connected with the minority by ancient ties, and by the memory of many a well fought battle in the present Assembly in defence of the old constitution. Last of all came Mr. Howe, the head and front of the party, which had effected all these changes, and who could not be denied a post in the Council opened to other members of his party. This provided places for three of the majority, but the other six members of the Council were men who had been in office since the earliest introduction of Representatives from the Assembly, and who were identified with the resistance made to these changes. The fact of Mr. Howe's consent to enter a cabinet so constituted, where it was impossible that his views could be carried out, indicates either a want of that clear conception of Responsible Government which he afterwards attained, or that he was impressed with the necessity of accepting any concession that could be wrung from the party of the Council. That the experiment turned out unsuccessful, was no more than might reasonably have been anticipated, but its eventual failure only shewed the necessity of adopting in their entirety the principles of party government which are the foundation of Responsible Institutions. In the meantime a general election was at hand. The House which had risen in the spring, had been elected for seven years, but had voluntarily shortened the term of its existence by a quadrennial Bill, which had been passed, but which was not to come into operation till the Royal assent was given to it. In June 1840 this assent was given by order in Council and it was soon afterwards made public in the newspapers. Forthwith preparations began for a General Election which came on in November. The elections were fought on the old principles. There was the party of the Council and the party of the Assembly, but from the compromise effected by the entry of three of the members of the Liberal majority into the Council, the battle was of a different character from that of 1830, or that of 1837. Of the old members twenty-seven were returned. No man of any mark was lost from those who were in the old House, and scarcely any man who afterwards rose to eminence appeared in the fresh material of which the twenty-two new members was composed

Mr. Archibald was returned for Colchester without opposition.

CHAPTER IX.

New Speaker. Reasons for Mr. Archibalds disqualification. Other Candidates equally disqualified. Two members of same Government contending for Speakership. Mr. Uniacke a member of Government moves resolution touching repeal of Union with Cape Breton. Resolution complimentary to Mr. Archibald adopted unanimously. Offered offices of Master of Rolls and Judge of Admiralty Court. Accepts. Mr. Archibald as Judge. Address at Truro. His Country seat. His habits at Truro. Hospitality. His Humour.

When the new House met on the 3rd February, their first act was of course to choose a Speaker. Mr. Archibald was no longer eligible for the chair. It had been made one of the terms of the new arrangement that the holder of the Crown office was not to be Speaker. Mr. Archibald had therefore to make choice between the two offices, and naturally preferred the Attorney Generalship which gave him a salary of $2,500, to the Speakership which yielded but $800. The reason assigned for making the Attorney General ineligible to the chair, was, that the holding of the two offices by the same person was inconsistent with British practice. No Attorney General in England, for a century past, had presided over the House of Commons. As the organ of the House, and its servant, the Speaker should be free from the influence of the Crown. His duty to the Commons might conflict with his obligation to the Sovereign. His paramount duty was the protection of the privileges of the House over which he presided. It was unsound in principle to place him in a position towards the Crown which would hamper him in the discharge of this special duty. The reasoning was sound, and Mr. Archibald was excluded. But the principle so announced, was applicable to all servants of the Crown, to a Cabinet Minister as well as to

an Attorney General. All such officials owe obligations
to the Sovereign that may conflict with the duty which a
Speaker owes to the Assembly. If to be a ministerial
servant of the Crown, was incompatible with the Speakership, *à fortiori*, the position of a Cabinet Minister who is
a higher servant, more liable to the influence of the
Crown, by direct and personal communication with its
representative, ought to disqualify the holder. But Mr.
Archibald was no longer a candidate for the position, and
of the three other gentlemen who aspired to the chair,
one only was not open to this objection. Mr. W. Young
was neither Minister nor Crown Officer, but, though
named at first, he soon found there was no chance of
success and withdrew. The choice then lay between
two other gentlemen who were quite as much disqualified
as Mr. Archibald. They were Mr. Howe and Mr. Uniacke,
both members of the Ministry, both advisers of the Lieutenant Governor. Not only so, but if English practice
was to prevail, the question of the Speakership is always
one of party. The candidate of the Government is put
forward as a test of strength in the House. But in this
case the Cabinet had no united policy. The personal
rivalries of two members of the Ministry, threw the
Speakership open to a scramble, which might have resulted in the selection of an opponent of Government.
In the end the House were nearly evenly divided. Twenty five members voted for Mr. Howe, twenty two for Mr.
Uniacke. Thus, in the very first step taken, under the
new regime, was displayed the gross inconsistency of
excluding from the chair one gentleman who had filled
it to the entire acceptance of the House for sixteen years,
and at the same time making a choice between two others,
both of whom should have been excluded on precisely sim-

ilar grounds, and who besides if not so disqual'fied, should
not have been found in antagonism on a Government
question. But then it must be remembered, that while
there were many gentlemen who had no official salary,
Mr. Archibald had two; and it is not in these latter days
only that the *pretext* sometimes differs from the *reason.*

Mr. Archibald's removal to the floor of the House
relieved him from the trammels of the chair. During
the Session of 1841 we find him taking a more prominent
part than of late in the discussions of the House. Several
of the speeches delivered by him during the Session give
abundant evidence of the vigor of his intellect, and of his
peculiar command of playful and appropriate illustration.
There was a question before the House this Session
which shewed how little the principles of the British
constitution were appreciated, or at all events acted
upon, when it was convenient to ignore them. Mr.
Uniacke had been returned one of the members for Cape
Breton, which had now, for twenty years, formed a county
of Nova Scotia. He was a leading member of the new
Government, and a sworn adviser of the Crown, and yet
on the 7th April, he rose in his place in the House and
moved a resolution for the dismemberment of the
Province. This resolution asserted the illegality of the
annexation of Cape Breton to Nova Scotia by the Crown
in 1820. Imagine a leading member of the Imperial
Ministry rising in the House of Commons to offer a
resolution setting forth that the annexation of Ireland in
1800 was contrary to law. Mr. Uniacke's resolution was
discussed at great length, and with much ability, and yet
not one of the speakers appears to have been struck with
the idea of the incongruity of such a proceeding on the
part of Mr. Uniacke, with his position as a member of

the Cabinet. A question of such magnitude, one touching the very integrity of the Province, was treated as if it were a matter of so trivial a moment that every member of the Cabinet could speak about it, and vote upon it, as he thought fit. The Attorney General made an able and eloquent speech against the resolution offered by his colleague, and towards the close of the debate Mr. Howe gave it the coup de grace, by declaring the whole proceeding one of the broadest of farces, and that too apparently without perceiving that the most absurd feature of the whole business, was the conduct of the Government, and particularly the section of it under his control, who, assuming to be great sticklers for British practice, were violating in their treatment of this subject the very fundamental principles of a Responsible Ministry. But the political exigencies of the moment underlay the whole thing, as they did in the case of the Speakership. One member of the Ministry wanted a salary, another a cry. So a Speakership was won by the first movement, and a constituency secured by the second. Both these could be done with safety. The Attorney General had to yield to one of the projects and to fight the other, while the new Speaker put an extinguisher on Mr. Uniacke's resolution by denouncing it as a screaming farce. The House appears to have felt some compunction for having been made parties to the adoption of a principle in one case, that they did not apply to another. At all events just before the close of the Session they passed an unanimous resolution in reference to their old Speaker, in which they declared their high sense of the faithfulness, ability and urbanity with which he had discharged for sixteen years the high and onerous duties of the chair: and Mr. Speaker was directed to announce the terms of the resolution to Mr. Archibald in his place of the House.

It was a graceful compliment and well deserved, and, as it happened, it came at a fitting time. It was the last act of a Session which wound up Mr. Archibald's connexion with political life. Five days after the close of the House, the death of Mr. Fairbanks caused a vacancy in the offices of Master of the Rolls and Judge of the Court of Vice Admiralty. Lord Falkland immediately offered the offices to Mr. Archibald. They had both, many years before, been offered to and refused by him, but times had changed. There was no longer a Chief Justiceship to aspire to. The occupant of that office, if older than himself, was at all events in vigorous health, and would probably, as he actually did, outlive him. The Judge had never been obliged to undergo the struggles of a political career in the Assembly, and he bade fair to hold office for many a year to come. Mr. Archibald, on the contrary, found his constitution seriously impaired by the incessant and harrassing labors connected with his position, and having now had thirty-five years' experience of political life, might reasonably be content with the part he had played, and accept the ease and dignity of the Bench for the closing years of his life. His friends urged this course upon him, and yielding at last to their suggestion, and to the dictates of his own judgment, he decided to accept the offer. Accordingly, on the 29th April he was sworn in as Master of the Rolls, and as soon afterwards as communication could be had with the Imperial authorities, he received the Admiralty commission.

From this time, in the pursuit of our narrative, we are freed from the necessity of entering into political

details. Hitherto our story could not be understood
without some explanation of the incidents of current
politics. Now, these were just beginning to assume a
most interesting appearance, but our course diverges
from them, and we must henceforth bid them adieu.

Mr. Archibald entered on the discharge of his judicial
duties, after a long training at the Bar in the principles
of his profession, and after an experience of four years
in the highest judicial office in Prince Edward Island,
but many members of the Nova Scotia Bar had their
misgivings as to how he would succeed in his new position.
There were some of the plodding members of that profession, who believed there could not be much wisdom
where there was so much wit, who thought that the
qualities of mind, and speech, which charmed juries, and
won verdicts, would not be found joined to the solid
judgment and logical faculties which were required in
the judicial seat. But they were much mistaken. Mr.
Archibald's mind was well stored with legal principles.
He had read and studied when people were giving him
credit only for playing and feasting. He was certainly
a man of most decided talent, and yet one of his maxims
was that no talent was so valuable as the talent of
industry. It is true he was very quick in seizing the
strong points of a case. A very slight examination of
his brief and of the law was all that he required. But
this examination he seldom, if ever, omitted. Thus he
appeared always thoroughly prepared. On one occasion
he had failed to make proper research before an argument came on in which he was the leading counsel. His
junior, however, had made up a capital brief, and just as
the cause was about to be called (this story is told by
the junior who now fills a high judicial position in the

Province), Mr. Archibald asked to glance at the brief.
It was handed to him—he ran his eye over it, and, taking
in the whole thing at a glance, he delivered one of the
most able arguments ever addressed to the Court, upon
the materials thus suddenly submitted to his notice. The
junior found his whole argument exhausted by the address of the leading counsel, and he says himself that he
took care thenceforth to reserve his thunder for his own
use.

Mr. Archibald soon had an opportunity of display-
ing his judicial qualities in his new position. The sound
common sense which distinguished his judgments, and
which, after all, forms the foundation of law and equity
—the clearness and precision with which the principles
underlying the case were announced and applied, gave a
character to his Decrees which was not generally expected on the part of the Bar. Had he ascended the Bench
earlier in life he would undoubtedly have left behind him
a reputation as a jurist not inferior to that of almost any
of the distinguished men who have held office as Judges
in Nova Scotia. Soon after his promotion he paid his
annual visit to the place with which so many of the associations of his life were connected. He owned a beautiful estate at Truro on the north side of Salmon River.
It was partly upland, partly intervale. The upland was
separated from the intervale by a steep bank, near the
edge of which stood his house, looking out on the level
plain in front, which was under the highest cultivation,
and studded with gigantic elms—many of them remnants
of the original forest, and all coeval with the first inhabitants of the Valley. Through these the beautiful
river meandered in graceful curves, which reflected the
western sun of a summer's afternoon in gorgeous hues.

A lovelier scene than that from the old homestead of Mr.
Archibald, Nova Scotia does not afford. His affections
clung to it from his youth upwards. Here every summer
he spent the leisure weeks he was able to steal from a
busy life, here he cultivated the kindly affections of his
neighbors, here he acquired by genial and unaffected
familiarity with the country people, that hold upon their
hearts which he retained to the end of his life. Here too,
he kept open house for all comers, who were delighted by
his courtesy, and charmed by his unfailing spirits. Here
he entertained the best and the noblest in the land. The
Dalhousies, the Kempts, the Foxes, as well as the simpler
inhabitants of the Country, shared his hospitality and
sang his praises. To this delightful spot he made his
way soon after his appointment to the Bench; and here
he found himself surrounded by friends who expressed
their welcome in an affectionate address. They con-
gratulated him upon his recent appointment—they
alluded to the various offices he had filled at home and
abroad—and in reference to their being sometimes the
gift of the people, and sometimes the gift of the sovereign,
they observed how acceptably he had discharged his
duties alike to Queen and subject, and finally they alluded
to the crowning act of his public career, when the
Assembly no longer permitted to elect him to their
chair, had passed the encomium, to which we have
referred, on his conduct while at their head. They expressed their hope that his new position would enable him
to spend more of his time among them. His reply is in
the affectionate strain proper to the occasion—he con-
cludes it by telling them that the kind welcome they had
given him would cement the attachments which made
the charm of social life. Among the people with whom

or with whose fathers his boyhood had been spent he was always received with delight. Those who did not know him personally knew him well by the stories that were told at the hearthstones of their parents. Wherever he went he was received with the greatest cordiality. It was his delight to take little excursions in the neighborhood, making up a party and driving to a sequestered spot, where a pleasant stroll could be had, or a picnic partaken of by a running stream—or in a shady grove. On these occasions his whole heart was in the excursion. He talked, and laughed, and told stories, and made jokes about anything and everything. The incidents of an afternoon's drive might be of the tamest and dullest character, but when he returned home, and had occasion to amuse others, who were not of the party, by a narrative of what had occurred, he would clothe the events in such a ludicrous garb, and that too without varying from the strictness of fact, that he convulsed with laughter, not only his new auditors, but the very persons who had been witnesses of the events, but who had certainly been unconscious of their absurdity till they heard him tell the story. It was this marvellous capacity for extracting fun out of anything and everything which made him so charming a companion. When he told a story it was a perfect play—he looked the character he personated—he had such a marvellous command of face that he could in an instant put on the features and air of the person he was talking about. He could use the exact dialect and voice, and the personation was so perfect, and the effect so irresistible, that everybody was carried away with it. We doubt if ever a better story teller existed in Nova Scotia. He seldom told the same anecdote twice, at all events to the same audience. He had a most marvellous repertory of odd things, and many of the best of them found their way into the pages of Mr. Slick, who appreciated and appropriated them. An instance occurred at his own table in Halifax, which showed the wonderful power he had of convulsing his auditors by his stories. At his dinner table there were about a dozen gentlemen who were his special friends. Soon the cheer began to be felt. Joke followed joke, queer story after queer story was told. Mr. Archibald took his full share, laughed at other people's jokes and made them laugh in return, till at last he hit upon a story so absurd and ludicrous, and told it in a way so utterly irresistible, that the guests were seized with convulsions of laughter so uncontrollable, that not one of them could retain his seat. By a simultaneous movement, the whole party, host and guests, were on their feet in a perfect ecstasy of excitement. But this was in his younger days, or at all events before advancing years and shattered health had sobered his wit to a more decorous tone.

CHAPTER X.

Success as a Judge. Failing health. Death. Meeting of Bar
Society. Speech of Chief Justice. Address of Condolence.
Meeting of Colchester people on his death. Eulogium of Mr.
Howe. Examination of charges against Mr. Archibald as a
public man. Mr. Howes views upon them. Mr Archibald in
his social relations. Death of his first wife. Account of his
second wife. Sir Charles Pollack and Sir T. D. Archibald.
Mr. Archibald's love for the sacred Scriptures. Anecdote relat-
ed by Rev. Mr. Morton. Thoughts of writer in concluding
Memoir.

The judicial duties of the Master of the Rolls, unlike
those of a Judge of a Common Law Court, were not of a
nature to bring him prominently before the public eye.
In the quiet business of the Court of Equity, his public
were mainly the members of the profession. They soon
began to see that successful as Mr. Archibald had been
in other walks of life, he was to exhibit qualities not less
high in the discharge of the duties of his new position.
There were some cases involving nice and difficult questions with which he had soon to deal, but he disposed of
them rapidly. In these he showed an amount of legal
lore and of solid judgement for which many members of
the Bar were unprepared, who formed their opinion of
him from the lighter qualities which had made so conspicuous a feature of his forensic speeches. The series of
decrees pronounced by him during the five years he sat
on the Bench, form a record of which no Judge would
need to be ashamed. Had he been made a Judge at an
earlier period and devoted to the duties of the Bench the
energies he had lavished on other pursuits, there cannot
be a doubt that he would have left behind him a name as
a jurist not inferior to that which he has left as an advocate and as a politician. But his health was much shattered by his previous labors, and when he ascended the

Bench he was not able to enter on his new pursuits with
the zeal and energy he had displayed at the Bar and in
the Assembly. For some years, with little apparent
change in his health, he continued to discharge, quietly but
regularly, the duties of his Court. His family could not
however but be apprehensive of the recurrence of
another attack of the same kind as he had suffered from
before, which would probably be fatal. At last the event
occurred which they had so much reason to fear. On
Wednesday evening the 28th January 1846, he was seated
at table with his wife and one or two members of his
family, and was in the act of drinking a cup of tea when
the expression of his face suddenly changed. He rested
his head for a moment on his hand, and then fell forward,
but was caught as he fell, and gently lowered to the floor.
In a few seconds it was found that all was over. The
spark of life had become extinct. It was a sad, but could
hardly be said to be an unexpected, close of his life. His
death was deeply felt by all classes. The House of Assembly was then in Session. Mr. Johnstone, who was
Attorney General at the time brought the mournful event
to the notice of the House in appropriate terms. Other
leading members spoke in a similar strain. It was resolved unanimously that the House should adjourn over
Saturday and attend the funeral in a Body. The Bar
Society held a meeting on hearing of the death. The
Chief Justice, the old friend, and the old and successful
rival, of the deceased, presided. He opened the meeting
in words creditable alike to his heart and his head—he
referred to the "amiable disposition, the amenity and
self command which characterized his departed friend,
while at the Bar, where he never permitted the warmth
of a contending counsel to wound the feelings of his oppo-

nent, or to transgress those rules which regulate the intercourse between gentlemen.   The younger members of the
Bar who remembered him more as the Judge than as the
Barrister would long cherish the recollection of his courteous demeanor, and unwearied patience; but both the
older, and the younger members of the profession, would
unite in admiring the talent, and the discrimination he displayed in the decrees which he pronounced while he ad-
orned the Bench, on which we should see him no more."

Suitable resolutions were passed, expressing the esti-
mation of the Bar Society of his high qualities, and offering their condolence to the family on this melancholy
occasion.   The Society decided to attend the funeral in a
Body. and in deep mourning.

In his own County, where he was so much loved
there was a meeting of a number of the leading inhabitants
who passed Resolutions in reference to the deceased, in
the sense of those of the Halifax Bar.

Now that he was no more, the feeling was universal
that a great man had descended to the grave.   Nova
Scotians of every grade and every creed were proud
to call the man that had passed away their fellow
countryman.   His reputation was then fresh.   The events
in which he had figured so prominently were within living memory.   Everybody knew the deceased, either personally, or by reputation.   The leading incidents of his
life were familiar to thousands.   The time that had
elapsed since he took an active part in life was enough to
mellow, not enough to efface, the recollection of the
scenes in which he had mingled.   Everybody had anec-
dotes about him – what he had done, what he had said.
The stories he had told, his wit, his humor, his kind deeds,
his courtesy, his polish of manner, all came back to

memory with a freshness which testified how dear he had made himself to the mass of his fellow countrymen.

We have had occasion to speak of the divergence which had taken place before the close of the House elected in 1830 between himself and Mr. Howe, the new leader of Young Nova Scotia. This divergence, in sentiment, if not always in action, had continued to increase up to the time of Mr. Archibald's accession to the Bench; but, when the grave had closed over his remains, all this was forgotten. Mr. Howe, in the columns of his newspaper, paid a tribute to the memory of the deceased in language so forcible and apposite that we cannot forbear to quote it, as a monument to the generosity and kind heartedness of the writer, as well as to the ability and worth of the deceased. Mr. Howe had opportunities of knowing Mr. Archibald which few other men enjoyed. He had in the Press sustained him when Speaker, in the great fight of 1830. He had supported him when he went to the county on the dissolution of the House in that year. He had rejoiced in the triumphant return of the men pledged to support Mr. Archibald's cause. He had, year by year, from his place in the gallery of the Assembly, where he sat taking notes of the proceedings and debates, watched the course taken by Mr. Archibald during the whole period from 1830 to 1837. In the latter year he had himself gone into the Assembly, and was in familiar and daily communication with him up to 1841, when Mr. Archibald went on the Bench.

There can therefore be no question as to Mr. Howe's opportunities of knowing thoroughly the character and qualities of the object of his sketch, and from what we have seen of the differences between the two men, it is impossible to ascribe the opinions he uttered to the partiality of unreasoning friendship.

" If," says Mr. Howe. "If the manners the temper or the intellect of a country were to be judged by a single specimen culled from the mass of its population, we know of no man to whom all eyes would have so naturally turned, to produce upon strangers a favorable impression, as to him who was followed to the grave by his fellow citizens on Saturday last. We speak not of Mr. Archibald as he appeared for the last two or three years, stricken by disease, and laboring under a paralysis of the muscles which disturbed the expression of his face, and at times rendered articulation difficult, if not impossible, but we speak of him as we knew him in the flower of his manhood, in the full possession of his faculties, the ornament of the Bar, the master spirit of the Senate and the felicitous humourist of the Social Circle. That " we shall ever look upon his like again" appears to us very improbable, for we often saw him surrounded by able men, none of whom presented so rare a combination of intellectual and agreeable qualities, and we look round upon our own contemporaries and do not find his equal.

We need not volunteer a biographical sketch of Judge Archibald, for the incidents of his early career and of his brilliant public life are familiar to his countrymen. Born in an humble sphere, his genius rose above vulgar prejudices, and even when elevated to the highest public positions, his purse was as open to the poor, as his heart was to all those sympathies from which spring enlarged legislation, dedicated to the general good. Almost self-educated, and, perhaps, profound upon no single topic, his range of information was extensive, and his wit often breathed the spirit disencumbered of the rubbish of classic lore. Bred among peasants, and trained in his youth to mechanical employment, his person was remarkably handsome, and his manners polished and unrestrained. Tried by every vicissitude of Provincial public life, his buoyant spirits never forsook him, nor did the crisis which ripened the judgment harden the heart.

*   *   *   *   *   *   *   *   *

"Circumstances made him often a courtier, and official employment made him the guardian of the prerogative, yet he was for years the darling of a popular Assembly, and while discharging the onerous duties of an officer of the Crown, rarely forgot that he was the Representative of the People. There were more laborious men than Mr. Archibald, both at the Bar and in the Assembly, but he generally outshone them all, by a tact that was almost instinctive, a discretion that seldom erred, a flowery elocution that never offended good taste, and homeliness, yet brilliancy, of wit, the native growth of the country, and adapted to its humor, by which an opponent, when most in the right, was often driven from the field and made to split his sides at his own discomfiture. It may be that we were over partial to our countryman, but we often looked around the benches of Congress, of the British Parliament, and of the Canadian Legislature for a man combining so many of the points of a brilliant and polished orator, but looked in vain. A more dignified and imposing Speaker we never saw in the chair of any Legislative Assembly.

That Mr. Archibald was not deeply read in law used to be said by the dull book worms of the profession who measure the extent of a man's acquirements by the hours he pores over a volume, rather than by the ideas he snatches from it in the scanty leisure of a busy life—but since his elevation to the Bench, his decisions have been on all hands acknowledged to have been as profound as they were upright and impartial. He has discharged since 1841 the duties of Master of the Rolls and Judge of the Court of Vice Admiralty with credit to the country and satisfaction to the Bar.

"But it was chiefly as he stood before us on the floors of the Assembly, as the leader of that great popular movement which convulsed the country in 1829, and which prepared the way for the final onslaught on the old system of Government, that we have ever delighted to contemplate the deceased. Then it was that with all the power and influence of the compact arrayed to crush him, with a hostile Governor, a determined Council, a shattered revenue and sheaves of misrepresentations going to Downing Street by every mail, and sorely tried by domestic sorrows, he took his stand upon the privileges of the People's House, and with a luminous eloquence and power of sarcasm, which we have seldom seen equalled and never surpassed, formed and controlled the public opinion which sent him back at the head of a triumphant majority, the advanced guard of that still more triumphant majority which was to complete the work he had so materially advanced.

"We have left ourselves but little space to speak of Judge Archibald as he appeared to his friends in the social circles where he ever shone. Those who have seen him at the head of his own table, or shared the enjoyment of his fireside, need not be reminded of the ease with which he threw aside the cares and labors of life, as a knight of old threw off his armor when the battle was over, and indulged in the merriment of the hour with the vivacity of a wit, and the playfulness of a child. His jests were endless, and his stories, nearly all of them Provincial, inimitable.

"Though ever so often heard, the variations and the luminous play of feature and expression of eye, made one fancy that the last was always the best. There was no venom or malignity about Judge Archibald—to give pleasure, and to share it, was a necessity of his nature, but it never gave him pleasure to give others pain. Light be the turf and cheerful the flowers above his head— we may almost venture to predict that no thorn will grow upon his grave."

These eloquent and graceful words bear the mark of genuine sincerity. Mr. Howe was not given to flattering either the living or the dead. The man whose memory could evoke from him such an eulogium as this, must have been no ordinary person. We have heard Mr. Howe in later life, express himself in similar language.

Different as were these two men in many respects, there were some points of resemblance between them. Each had an original and creative mind. Each had a marked and striking individuality. Nobody could mistake a speech of Mr. Archibalds', or an editorial of Mr. Howe, as the production of the other or of any third person. In each case the stream bore evidence of the source from which it flowed. In each, the features of the offspring betrayed the paternity. Both men were self made and largely self taught; they had been bred to different lines of pursuit, but each had his special object of ambition. The lawyer had hoped to reach the head of his profession, the layman had set his heart on filling the highest position in Nova Scotia open to lay ambition. They were both, in one sense, disappointed. The lawyer never sat in the Chief Justice's chair. The layman became Governor, but only to die. Both had had brilliant and successful careers—both had broken down from excessive toil. For some time before the close of their lives, both were mere wrecks of their former selves. They were both able and eloquent men. It is true they differed, widely as the poles, in manner and style, in appearance and address, and yet they resembled each other in one striking respect. Of all the men who have flitted across our political stage, no others ever attained such a hold as did these two, on the hearts and affections of Nova Scotians.

The remains of Mr. Archibald were interred in the Camp Hill Cemetery at Halifax, where a marble monument marks the place of sepulture.

In looking back on our memoir we fear that we shall be charged with the usual vice of biographers. It will be said that we have composed an eulogium, not written a life. We shall be asked how it is that when writing of a man who so long played a prominent part in the politics of this country, of one who was constantly assailing, and being assailed by, political opponents in no measured terms, how it is we have said so little of the charges brought against him by his political antagonists. To this we may answer in the first place, generally, that compared with those brought against public men, even in our own day, these charges are of little account. We gather them from the press of the day, or from speeches made on the floor of the House, and yet, with all the exaggerations of passion and party spirit they are not of a very deep dye. It is said that his great vice was ambition—that to it he sacrificed everything—but when we seek for proof to justify the assertion we do not find it. Besides ambition is a vice only when its aims are inconsistent with the public good. The desire to occupy a prominent position—the wish for power to influence political action, is a laudable and useful feeling.

In what then was Mr. Archibald's ambition shewn that was injurious to his country ? His action as to the Quit Rents is one of the things most frequently brought as a charge against him in the press of the day. We have not entered in our narrative into the history of the Quit Rent question. All interest in it has long since passed away. We have, therefore, not felt it necessary to go into the various details which would have been required to render the action of the Legislature intelligible. So far as our present object is concerned, it is enough to say that on the original grants of lands in Nova Scotia a Quit Rent of 2s. per 100 acres was reserved to the Crown. For many years after the settlement of the Province no attempt was made to collect it. Afterwards, from time to time, instructions came from the Colonial Ministers directing its enforcement. These were met by remonstrances from the Assembly which led to various postponements, the collection still always being threatened. Eventually a bill was passed commuting the Rents for a fixed sum given to the Crown in lieu thereof. Year after year Mr. Archibald spoke and voted in favor of this commutation. The reasons he gave had great force. They were sufficient at last to prevail on the Assembly, which for many years had fought against the settlement, finally to agree to it, as the best thing that could be done in the public interests. Mr. Archibald was Attorney General when the Bill passed. His salary, as such, was derived from the Crown revenue, and this was hardly sufficient to meet the charges upon it. The grant of £2,000 a year in lieu of Quit Rents went to swell that revenue. It thereby became better able to meet the burdens borne upon it, and the charge against Mr. Archibald was that his advocacy of the measure

originated, not in the public interest, but in the private
and personal interest he had in the Crown revenue being
made sufficient to meet the salaries borne upon it—his
own among the number—but it was not pretended that
his salary was too high, or that it ought to have been, or
would otherwise have been, unpaid. It could hardly be
considered for the public good that the tax gatherers
should be let loose among the people of the Province, to
collect from every owner of 100 acres the 2s. a year due
upon his land. The charge amounts to this, that the
policy advocated by Mr. Archibald, though really the
best in the public interest, incidentally increased the fund
from which his salary was paid. We have seen the
answer made by himself to the charge in his speech at
the hustings, at Truro, in 1836.

The most serious charge brought against him was
the one touching the erection of the Court of Common
Pleas. We have already mentioned the legislation on
this subject. An Act was passed in the first instance to
establish a Court of the kind in the Island of Cape Breton.
1t was rumored at the time that this Act was intended to
provide a place for Jared I. Chipman, Esq., who had been
a favorite member of the Assembly, but who had lost his
seat, and was then Sheriff of the County of Halifax.. If
this report were well founded, the Act did not effect its
object, for Sir James Kempt took the matter into his own
hands and appointed Mr. Marshall to the office. Next
year, however, another Act was brought in to extend the
system to Nova Scotia. The Province was divided into
three districts, and power was given to appoint a Judge
in each. By this means it was supposed that provision
was being made for Mr. Chipman who was not in the
House, and for Mr. Ritchie and Mr. Haliburton who were.

At the same time Mr. Robie, the Speaker, was to be elevated to the Council and made Master of the Rolls. A salary for him as such was provided by another Act. All this legislation took place, so said the press of the day, to enable Mr. Archibald to step into the chair as Speaker when Mr. Robie retired to the Rolls, and Mr. Haliburton and Mr. Ritchie to the Bench. The absurdity of this story is its best refutation. The various offices were certainly created, and appointments made to them, but to suppose all this to have been done in furtherance of the objects and schemes of any one man, is to suppose what is simply incredible. Whether the statutes creating the Courts were wise or not is a different question. We are disposed to think they were not. Public opinion was never favorable to the new Courts. It soon became very adverse, and eventually the Courts were abolished—but we must not forget that there is another side to the question, and that the same Courts, or something very similar, were long afterwards found to be necessary. That they were created and now exist, and are doing a useful work. There were several grounds for the hostility to the first Inferior Courts. A large sum was thereby thrown upon a Treasury not able to bear it. With Mr. Robie's salary it amounted to $7,000 a year. This sum all went into the pockets of a profession which did not stand in the best odor at the time. It was an additional objection that the Bill was carried in the Assembly by a majority of only one, and would not have been carried but for the votes of the very men who were to fill the offices their votes created. Whether the Bill was right or wrong, it cannot be doubted that the mode in which it was carried gave a great shock to the public conscience. This of itself is sufficient to account for the unpopularity of the Courts. It does not follow by any means that the policy was unsound, or the Courts unnecessary.

Then, again, it was asserted that Mr. Archibald's action at the time of the Brandy question in 1830 was not only due to pique, but was inconsistent with the opinions he had expressed when, as Chief Justice of Prince Edward Island, the same question came up for the consideration of the Council over which he then presided. We have already in the course of our narrative examined that part of the charge which ascribes his action to temper. As to the question of consistency, we are disposed to admit that there was a considerable divergency between the views he entertained on the question at the different times referred to, but a change of opinion on such a subject, very natural under the circumstances, is perfectly consistent with conscientious convictions. All these matters were discussed in the celebrated letters which appeared during the summer of 1836, over the signature of Joe Warner, and to which we have already adverted. The charges were set forth with great force of language, in every form of invective and sarcasm. They were supported by voluminous quotations from the Public Records. The letters produced, as we have already had occasion to say, a powerful effect all over the Province. They operated on public opinion in Mr. Archibald's own county, and that, too, though the author was obliged to admit that Colchester owed much to its member for the great benefits which his influence in the Assembly enabled him to confer on it. But, after all, what do these charges one and all amount to, compared with those that have been made against every public man of eminence in our day? On the whole we are inclined to think that a passage in the article by Mr. Howe from which we have already made some quotations, a passage which we purposely omitted at the time with a view to citing it here, gives a condensed but correct view of the matter of which we are now writing.

"He had," says Mr, Howe, "his faults like other men, but the only one we can remember which in the eyes of his countrymen seemed to detract from his merits, and sometimes laid him open to the shafts of political opponents, was a disregard of economy in public expenditure. This was about the only point on which ourselves and others who highly esteemed him were constrained at times to diverge from his usual currents of thought. But, if sometimes too lavish to public servants, it cannot be doubted that he had confident reliance on the growing resources of his country, the development of which he endeavored to stimulate by a liberal public expenditure."

Where is the man at this day who has spent 35 years in the Commons House—all the time, or nearly all, either moulding or greatly influencing the action of the Assembly—who is open to no charge more serious than a "disregard of economy in public expenditure"— qualified by the admission that by that means "he endeavored to "stimulate the development of the growing resources of. the country?"

As to political charges, therefore, his adversaries really had few to bring against him, and these not very serious. As to private or personal charges, none exist. A more blameless private life is not to be found in our history. The kindliness of his feelings made him extend his care for others whose interests were in his hands beyond the period of his own life. His will contains a clause directing his executors to be indulgent to his debtors, and not to distress them unnecessarily in enforcing the collection of the amounts due by them. Upon the whole, therefore, we have no apology to make for presenting the subject of our Memoir in a favorable light. We should not have the courage of our convictions if we did not assert what we believe, after a study of his life, embracing a great many incidents and events which we have not felt it necessary to relate. We are convinced that no son of Nova Scotia has proved himself more worthy of esteem and respect for all that is good and amiable, or more worthy of admiration for talents and statesmanship, than he whose life and career we have endeavored faithfully to describe.

In his social relations Mr. Archibald was eminently happy. His first wife was amiable, handsome and accomplished. She was distinguished for easy and gentle manners, and was a great favorite in society. She liked to have young people about her, and to see them enjoying themselves. She was, like her husband, always ready to take part in any innocent amusement. She brought him a large family. Five of her sons grew to manhood, and were young men about the time their father had become prominent in public life. They were able and clever men. Two of them still survive—the Consul General at New York, and Blowers Archibald of North Sydney. There were three daughters, all of whom are now deceased. At the time we are speaking of, Mr. Archibald's own residence was in the corner house opposite the old Mason Hall, and a pleasant house it was. The family was large enough to require little addition to make up a party. They were all cheerful and happy people. One of the sons played on the flute, another on the violin. A few young friends formed the circle—the old people entered into the spirit of the moment—a party was extemporised at any time—the music and the dance went on, and the most delightful reunions were thus made without effort and enjoyed without stint. Some persons, still living recall with enthusiasm scenes of the kind in which they took part over fifty years ago.

Mrs. Archibald died on the 13th May, 1830, at the age of 43. This was the year of the great fight over the Brandy question. It was in the very midst of the turmoil in which her husband was then involved, that this great blow fell upon him, and the grave closed over the remains of the mother of his children, and the beloved wife who had been his companion for a quarter of a century. The inscription on the family cenotaph in the Episcopal Church at Truro, which describes her as " amiable, gentle, charitable and sincere," and adding that she " passed her life on earth in the exercise of the Christian graces," says no more of her than is confirmed by the recollection of many now living, and by the traditions of Halifax society.

Mr. Archibald's second wife was Mrs. Brinley, the widow of an officer of the British Commissariat. She was a woman of high principle—in every respect an excellent person—but of a type and style entirely different from the first. She was not fond of society. She preferred the family circle -a few intimate friends rather than a great number of friendly acquaintances. She was systematic and methodical in her habits—active in every work of kindness and charity. Of her three children, who were all females, one died in infancy, a second died unmarried, the third became the wife of Sir Charles Pollock, Baron of the Exchequer in England,

a man of very considerable mark as a Judge in the High
Court of Justice. Thus it came to pass that two brothers-
in-law often went the circuit in England, presiding over
the same Courts, and attached to each other by the ten-
derest ties of personal regard, who were, one the son, and
the other the son-in-law, of the subject of our memoir.

As we have already stated, Mr. Archibald was of a race
that had been Presbyterian for many generations. The
family came originally from Scotland, and brought their
religious tenets with them. In early life he was bred a Presbyterian, and at one time, as we have said before, he had
some idea of entering the Ministry. His mind from
infancy had been deeply impressed with religious truth.
Like all men bred Presbyterians, he had a great
familiarity with the Bible. The pure Saxon of Holy
Writ was the model of his style, his words were plain and
clear, his meaning could never be mistaken—yet his
language was never bald. There was in his speeches a
poetic imagery that raised them above the level of mere
prose. Every speech he made showed his familiarity
with the sacred books. Seldom did he address the Assembly, or his constituency, or a jury, without making
some allusion, which showed how his fancy fed on the
beauties of the Holy Scriptures. The Psalms were his
favorite portion of the Bible. In family worship, which
he kept up in the latter years of his life, it was from the
Psalms that he selected his portion of Scripture for the
day—he read it in a tone of voice, which showed how
much he was carried away by the fervor and devotion of
the inspired writer, and when the prayer followed which
was an extempore effusion, suggested often by the passages that had just been read, he spoke in a tone so
reverend, in words so simple and earnest, that his prayer

seemed to breathe the very spirit of the sweet singer of Israel himself.

Mr. Archibald never took a conspicuous part in public religious exercises. We have therefore little to say of him in that respect. It would, however, hardly be right to omit mention of an incident related by the Rev. Roland Morton, an aged and well known Methodist Minister of high standing in the body to which he belongs. The incident would seem to have had its origin in the peculiar susceptibility of Mr. Archibald to religious emotion.

About the year 1826 (says Mr. Morton) a meeting was held on a Sunday morning in the old Presbyterian Church at Cornwallis. In the absence of the regular Minister it was presided over by the father of Mr. Morton who was an Elder of the Church. Mr. Archibald, who, it seems, was in the neighborhood at the time, but was not known personally, entered the church and took his seat among the audience. His professional dress might have been the occasion of the mistake, at all events he was supposed to be a clergyman, and, as was usual at that day, under such circumstances, he was invited by the presiding Elder to deliver an address. He hesitated for a little, but eventually rose to his feet, and to use Mr. Morton's language, " poured out from a heart evidently roused to its very depths, a gentle, sparkling, moving and solemn oration " which greatly affected the audience, who were excited to tears and sobs by his passionate and eloquent appeal." Using, as he always did, "the surrounding circumstances " for the illustration of his discourse, he pointed to the graves of the dead, seen through the windows, and made them the subject of some very interesting and affecting remarks.

The scene is painted in vivid colors by Mr. Morton who, after the lapse of fifty-five years, retains a recollection of the incident as lively as if it had occurred only yesterday. We think this was a singular exception to the rule laid down for himself in such cases. He was probably carried away by the excitement of the moment. There can be no doubt, however, that he would have achieved a great success in the pulpit, if he had persisted in his original idea of entering the Ministry.

We have now followed the subject of our Memoir from the cradle to the grave. We have endeavored to exhibit him as a lawyer, as a politician, as a judge. We have furnished some glimpses of his private life. We confess that the man has grown on our affections as we have proceeded with our narrative. We have sympathized with him in his early struggles. We have cheered him as he battled with his opponents. We have enjoyed his pleasures and shared his triumphs, and now that the time is come that we are to part with the companion of our journey who has grown dear to us, with whom we have acquired an intimacy which fellow travellers with kindred sympathies form on a long journey together— we confess to a feeling of regret that the journey is so near the end. We have found, too, that the materials for our history have grown under our hands. With the earlier incidents of the life of Mr. Archibald, we were little familiar when we began our narrative, and even as to later events, those which are within living memory, we had but a dim and confused recollection. It was only as they were connected with leading features of Provincial History that they were known to us at all. The more personal details had never been put in readable shape. They were deeply entombed in the records of the Legis lative Library ; buried in the 600 volumes of manuscript records, in the 1200 volumes of Nova Scotia newspapers, and in the 12,000 pamphlets which have been saved from destruction, mainly by the energy and industry of Dr. Aikins and Mr. J. T. Bulmer, both of whom deserve well of their country. Who shall undertake the task of quarrying from this rich mine the masses of pure ore which now lies hidden and buried in heaps of almost impenetrable rubbish ?

If our feeble efforts shall have been so far successful as to have rescued from the oblivion fast settling upon them, some incidents of an interesting life, we shall feel that our work has not been altogether in vain. Nova Scotia has had her fair share of able and eloquent men. Of some of these we have had glimpses as they flitted across the pages of our narrative. Many of them have done and said things which ought not to be forgotten, but so far as our judgment goes, there is no one of them, taking him for all in all, of whom Nova Scotia has greater reason to be proud, than of Samuel George William Archibald.

www.ingramcontent.com/pod-product-compliance
Lightning Source LLC
Chambersburg PA
CBHW031108020726
47495CB00007B/2096